Lip
Service

Lip Service

Edited by
Jenna Jameson
with
M. Catherine OliverSmith

SOUNDS PUBLISHING™

Savannah, Georgia

Text Copyright © 2008 Sounds Publishing, Inc.

Published by: Sounds Publishing, Inc.
             7400 Abercorn Street, Suite 705-300
             Savannah, GA 31406
             www.soundspublishing.com
             email: info@soundspublishing.com

Library of Congress Control Number: 2008922847

ISBN-10: 0-9799872-1-0
ISBN-13: 978-0-9799872-1-2

First printing: July 2008

Printed and manufactured in the United States of America

10   9   8   7   6   5   4   3   2   1

For additional information on *JennaTales, erotica for the woman on top* or to download audio erotica visit www.jennatales.com.

Distributed by Kensington Publishing Corp.

Submit Wholesale Orders to:
Kensington Publishing Corp.
c/o Penguin Group (USA) Inc.
Attention: Order Processing
405 Murray Hill Parkway
East Rutherford, NJ 07073-2316
Phone: 1-800-526-0275
Fax: 1-800-227-9604

*Just so everyone knows—and this isn't **lip service**—but having the opportunity to work with prolific, depraved, funny, sexy, and smart writers to build the **JennaTales** series is certainly some of the best fun I've had in my life. So this thank-you goes to the creative minds behind these amazing stories.*

Contents

Editor's Note

I haven't had this much fun since I don't know when. I mean law school was fun and all that (ha) but reading thousands of short erotic stories, culling the best for this series, and finally working with Jenna Jameson has been an amazing and incredible experience.

We launched the series with book signings and gallery-type events for the beautiful photographs by celebrity photographer Mike Ruiz. We hosted champagne red-carpet events on both coasts. We have had additional signings at book festivals and requests from all over the world for translations of the stories. It has been a whirlwind of a launch this year and it shows absolutely no signs of slowing down. And for that I am particularly thankful. I cannot imagine a more exciting and frantic time and I am loving every minute of it. I hope you are, too.

I love that the series is creating new fans for Jenna Jameson. I love that her die-hard longtime fans are so rapturous about the books. I get e-mails and notes daily from all over telling me how these crazy, sexy, funny, wonderful JennaTales have inflamed imaginations, livened up libidos, and helped people get all revved up and ready to rumble and tumble in the hay. I have people thanking us for including the sex tips, those precious nuggets of sexy knowledge that tell you how to do what, by all appearances, you very much want to do.

Jenna Jameson has been so amazing and supportive of the series, making suggestions for future titles, working with Mike Ruiz to capture the exact right look for our beautiful covers, beautiful because the two of them together make real art with his talent and her sensuality and sensational smile.

Of course, our writers are a wonderful group of depraved and wanton maniacs. I can barely keep up and we have more people wanting to write for the series each day. In fact, if you'd like to try your hand at writing a JennaTale, visit www.jennatales.com for information on how to submit your own story. While there, listen to a free audio erotic story and enjoy a little hands-free fun. We have seventy or so stories for you to download and listen to for immediate gratification or you can order CDs of stories as well.

Playboy Radio has been amazing with their support for the JennaTales series, playing the stories on satellite radio and letting more and more Jenna Jameson fans know about this great, sexy, fun series. We really appreciate all the shout-outs and support we have gotten for JennaTales.

Enjoy the stories and enjoy yourself.

As always,

—M. Catherine OliverSmith

Lip Service

Makes me long for a rainy day just so I can wear a slicker and get slicker.

First Trip to Paris

Pauline's nose and mouth were pressed against his ribs. Each breath she exhaled tickled his side. Stretching his arm over her head so that he could stroke her nape, she shivered.

"Paris!" she said, nipping the skin of his side with tiny, sharp teeth. "Paris makes me feel naughty." Her tongue flicked at the hard bud of his nipple.

"Everything makes you feel naughty."

"True." Rolling onto her back, she gave a great arms-stretched-high yawn. Her small soft elfin breasts lifted. He reached for one but she slithered out of bed and padded naked to the French windows of the room. Pauline threw open the doors and stepped, bare, onto the little square balcony.

"Paris wakes early," he told her. "People will see you."

"Lucky them," she called back. "Do you think someone might be looking at me right now?"

"I'm sure that half of Paris is looking." He tossed the sheet aside so that she could see his arousal if she cared to look back. "Why not come back to bed and inspire someone you know?"

She caressed her breasts, straining her neck to try to reach her mauve nipple with the tip of her pink, wet tongue. She lifted a leg, placing her foot up on the iron rail of the balcony, exposing herself to all of Paris. She licked her finger slowly, looking over her shoulder back at the bed. She leaned a little forward, enough to show him her spread sex as she reached her hand down and inserted her now-moistened finger into herself, drawing it out and pushing it back in several times before lowering her leg and licking her finger clean as she walked over slowly, reluctant to desert her theoretical audience. "Do you want me, Jamie?"

"It's been a full day since last I had you, Pauline. Of course I want you. I wanted you last night but you were too tired from the flight."

"I wasn't too tired," she said.

"Then why did you push me away?"

"Paris. Our first time in Paris. It has to be special."

"And what would make it special for you? Do you want us to make love on the balcony for the early risers to watch? Is it a special treat for the delivery boys on their bikes and the flower sellers setting up their carts that you wish?"

She shook her lovely head. "Nice thought. What a nicely vivid imagination you have. But, no, that would not be special enough. Not for Paris. Not for our first time in Paris."

"Then?"

"Keep wanting me, Jamie. Think about having me. Be ready and I'll tell you when, okay?"

"There's no problem there. I do want you. I always want you. But you've already got a plan, don't you?" Though spoken as an accusation, Jamie smiled as he thought of her planning something naughty and sexy.

"Of course I have a plan. When have I not? It is a fantasy but today, together, we'll make it a reality. I've been planning it, relishing it, feeling it ever since you showed me the tickets and told me you were bringing me to Paris. Are you ready to give it life, Jamie?"

Showing her his full arousal, Jamie's willingness was hugely apparent. "No time like the moment, Pauline. You could have told me the fantasy and I could have shared it with you these last weeks."

Giggling, Pauline touched a finger to the tip of his penis before she leaned in and whispered into his parted lips, "You'll share it when it happens."

She lowered her head and looked up at him through her lashes. "Now get ready. We have to go do tourist things."

"I thought we were doing something else."

"It looks like rain. I packed raincoats." Pauline tossed his on the bed, then, carrying her matching one over her arm, she walked to the bathroom, firmly closing the door behind her.

When they left, the rain was still in the low belly of the clouds. They found a bistro. Pauline, of course, selected an outdoor table. Whatever she had on under her long yellow slicker had to be incredibly short. She let the slicker part over one extended, toe-pointed, naked leg. A passing man tripped over the leash of his Pekinese. Jamie grinned across the table. "Bitch!"

Pauline gave him an innocent look. "No. I'm sure the dog was a boy."

By then she'd accumulated an audience; the slovenly waiter, arms crossed, leaning on the coffee machine; a man who pretended to do a crossword while peeking at Pauline's leg; two men who were supposed to be painting a storefront across the street, all openly staring, plus the slow-twisting necks of half the people passing by.

Pauline put a dab of raspberry preserve on the tip of her tongue, leaned across the table, and beckoned to Jamie. Arching over the table, Jamie slowly ate the morsel of jam from her mouth.

He said, "You've raised more than eyebrows, Pauline."

"I have? Show me a sample."

Standing, his coat over his arm, he made no effort to hide the bulge in his jeans.

Pauline clapped fingertips to her lips. "Ooh la la!"

Pauline stood. Her slicker fell into place, covering her leg. A couple of disappointed sighs resulted. "I'm ready for the tourist attractions now, Jamie. We're getting a cab to the Eiffel Tower."

Standing at the curb, Jamie failed to hail a taxi, watching in frustration as they passed by his waving arm. Pauline took one step into the road, with that long slender thigh showing once more, and got one immediately. As they rode, she held his erection through his jeans. He tried to slip a hand inside her coat, only to have her push his hand away.

Fat heavy raindrops spackled the windshield in twos and threes. As Jamie settled back, Pauline's hand located his zipper, tugging it down. She slipped her hand into his jeans, pulling him free. Warm fingertips drummed along Jamie's rigid shaft. She was playing softly with him. It became obvious that while she wanted him erect and engorged, Pauline had no intention of relieving the pressure, at least not immediately.

The cab lurched to a halt. Jamie went to tuck himself in and zip up, but Pauline leaned over and whispered, "Leave it just like that, Jamie. Nice and handy."

With his coat covering his erection, Jamie climbed from the cab, heavy cock wagging free. It was an odd, arousing sensation.

Under the shelter of the Eiffel Tower itself, Pauline put her hand back under his coat and grasped his still firm cock. She gazed up at Jamie, squeezing. "That's some club you have there, Jamie."

There was no line for the elevator due to the rain, though a few passengers joined them on their trip to the top. With only six others in the rather large cage, Pauline and Jamie were neither alone nor anonymous in a crowd. Despite this, Pauline slid her hand inside Jamie's raincoat once more. Her palm was slick.

"What is that on your hand?" Jamie asked as normally as possible.

In her free palm rested two packages of airline butter. "I came prepared, Jamie. I've been saving these and warming them nicely for just this occasion." Her other hand remained busy inside his coat.

The Eiffel's elevator gives a strange ride, rising at something of a diagonal at first. A man pushed a laden dolly off at the second stop. Two girls in tiny skirts pretended not to notice what Pauline's hand was doing to Jamie while a tall man watched from the corner of his eye. A couple, the woman plump and in her late forties, the man thin and fiftyish, watched more frankly.

When they arrived at the third level, Pauline extracted her hand, licking butter from her palm. "Come on."

His erection threatening to poke though the fly of his raincoat, Jamie followed. Running swift-footed around the deck, Pauline threw herself up onto a guardrail. It was high enough that her feet dangled a foot above the plank floor as she leaned on her belly.

"Careful! I don't want to lose you."

"Not a chance!"

Jamie put his hands on the girders, one to each side of her and close enough that her bottom pressed on his chest.

"See over there?" Pauline shouted with glee. "It's not raining at all."

In the distance, Paris was golden.

"I'm never going to forget this view," Pauline told him. "You are going to help me remember it, Jamie."

"I am? How?"

"My coat has a slit up the back. Part it and unbutton your coat. Come in very close now, Jamie."

With one hand Jamie unbuttoned his coat while the other investigated the slit in hers. He wasn't quite shocked to find her naked. His hand found skin, cool on her thighs, warmer on the cheeks of her bottom.

She turned her head. "Lower me," she said. "Do me, here and now."

Jamie wrapped his coat around her hips for some minimum concealment, not that there would be much doubt what they were doing. Pauline squirmed lower. His tip left a slippery trail as it nestled in the heat between her thighs.

"Now," she commanded.

Gripping Pauline's hips through his coat and her slicker, Jamie braced his legs and lowered her until his penis slipped inside. Pauline jerked back and down. She held on to the girder and twisted her upper body to get her mouth on his.

"Do it! Do it hard and deep."

Rain plastered her hair and sluiced down their faces, mingling in their mouths. Raising himself on his toes, Jamie drove his cock all the way up. Pauline squeezed him in a slow steady rhythm. "Yes, Jamie. You're fucking me on top of the Eiffel Tower. I bet we're the first. Come for me. Fill me. Don't hold back. I want to feel you inside me."

Jamie suddenly felt himself losing all control as his thighs thudded and he jolted into her. Pauline began to moan, then she convulsed, shuddered, and relaxed. Jamie came hard into her, throwing his head back, tasting the rain.

Jamie lowered her gently, almost reverently, and her slicker fell back into place. He tucked himself away, then, nonchalantly took Pauline's hand; together they walked back to the elevator.

Morgana Baron

JennaTip #1: Stiffy Lube

In the story, our powerfully sexy woman uses butter to lube up her man's member. While butter might feel nice and slick, it isn't recommended as a lubricant for intercourse because butter is a dairy product containing animal fat and it has bacteria in it that could lead to some funky and nasty infections. It can also degrade condoms, potentially causing them to fail. And you really don't want your condoms to fail. That's like having no brakes on a car going downhill in a snowstorm. Not a good experience.

Crisco shortening is man-made and not natural at all and has a long history of being used as a sexual lubricant since it hit the shelves back in the 1950s. While it's thick and very creamy and doesn't dry out, it is messy.With some dishwashing liquid mixed in with regular laundry detergent, rumor has it that any Crisco stains on whatever it's gotten on—sheets, towels, clothes, or your boyfriend's ex-wife's childhood blanket that he kept because she was such a nasty piece of work through the whole divorce—will come out. Again, Crisco should not be used with latex as it can cause the condom or other latex item to deteriorate.

Crisco may have a long history but do consider that while you may get it out of your clothes, you may have a hard time getting it out of your body, which could lead to some very funky and unsexy results.

Overall, just stick with the water-based lubricants that have been created specifically for the job at (or in) hand for best and safest results.

I imagine the shirt she's wearing is really one of his white business shirts with the cuffs rolled up.

Freed

"You're sure?" Jane felt awkward as she fastened the last leather cuff tightly around Mark's wrist. He smiled warmly. His dark brown eyes glanced up at the stained ceiling and then back to meet hers. Jane looked around at their tiny apartment with its mishmash of mainly found items.

The harsh light from the student lamp on the cluttered desk lit Mark's lithe body. He sat naked, bound to the frame of a hard wooden chair by his wrists, forearms, neck, thighs, and ankles. His dark wavy hair curled at his neck.

"Are you comfortable like that?" She couldn't stop looking at him, wondering how he didn't mind being so very exposed. Jane gripped the top of her shirt, squeezing the buttons in her hand as though they were magic talismans that would keep her safe and hidden.

"Leave your shirt on." Mark's voice was a gentle whisper. He saw the look of relief on her face. What a shame his beautiful woman was so self-conscious. He was chained up now, so she could be free. He'd be totally exposed and take all the risks.

"Leave your glasses on, too."

He gestured, with a lift of his chin, toward the ottoman sitting between his bound legs. "Come. Sit with me." The chains that were attached to his leather restraints clanked loudly. Mark's limbs were firmly bound. His chest heaved, stretching his rippling muscles over his ribs.

Jane clambered over his left leg carefully and sat on the stool between his legs. She tried not to stare at his large cock. Despite her passionate love for him there were times when she found it difficult to accommodate him. And despite that love or because of that love, Jane was terrified to let go of her control. Would he love her if she gave in to her wild desires? Would her fantasies disgust him? She was such a bundle of contradictions and worries. She didn't know how she had ended up so lucky to have such a compassionate and passionate lover and friend. Because he really was her friend and he really did love her, they were trying out an experiment to see if by binding him she could become unfettered by her conventions and find a way to experience sexual freedom.

"What do you want me to do?"

"Whatever you want." His voice was husky.

Mark looked at her sitting there self-consciously. She was his beautiful intellectual. A girl who loved ideas, wore glasses, and didn't know how sexy she was. Maybe these chains wouldn't work. Maybe she wouldn't unchain her mind just because he'd chained his body. God, how he wanted to just grab her shirt and rip it open, plunge his face between her ample breasts, feel her hair tickle across his body, and suck her until she loosened enough to take in all of him.

Jane watched fascinated as his manhood began to grow. A low moan came from his soft perfect lips. She felt a sudden heat between her legs. With a trembling hand she touched the soft dark hair on his right thigh. He gasped and closed his eyes. His cock stood up rock hard. She leaned in closer and blew her hot breath on his balls. The skin of his sack puckered and roiled. The mustiness of him filled her nostrils. Her mouth moistened and, without thinking, she clamped it over one of his soft shuddering testicles. She sucked softly, gently pulling its roundness into her mouth, savoring the salty warmth, the rasp of hair against her tongue. Mark moaned and pulled against his restraints. With her tongue she traveled over the soft valley between his balls and latched on to the left one, this time sucking it deeper in to her mouth. His thigh muscles rippled as he arched his back.

When his tight ass lifted up from the chair as he strained against the leather bindings, Jane slid her hands under and squeezed his hot damp cheeks as she continued to suck and pull his balls, this way and that, deep within her mouth. His breath was a rumbling animal pant.

Jane's nipples rose to rock-hard pebbles against the lace of her bra. Her pussy twitched with urgency. She slid her hands out from beneath him and gently released his balls from her mouth.

She looked at him. Mark was watching her. His face was wet with sweat. His erection was mammoth. But he was safely chained and strapped down. Jane could do whatever she liked. He had said so.

Jane felt for the top button of her shirt. Mark sucked in his breath as she slowly undid the button. With a shaking finger, she swiped the tip of his cock and rubbed the moisture between her breasts.

The skin of his dick was impossibly tight. He wanted to feel her snug, hot pussy expanding over it, but he had to suffer and wait for her to decide when and what was right. Slowly she began to undo the rest of the buttons. He couldn't wait to see her in this bright light, her gorgeous breasts swinging. He yanked on the chains, unable to stop the automatic physical response, the need to reach, to touch.

Jane threw the shirt to the floor and helped herself to the new bead of moisture that emerged from the tip of his cock. She rubbed it between her fingers and slid her hand under her bra.

"Please." His face had never looked so vulnerable.

Jane slowly reached back to unfasten her bra strap.

"Please. You're so beautiful." He could barely get the words out.

She looked down. Her breasts *were* beautiful. She hadn't really ever considered that before. Her skin felt a prickly chill as she grasped her nipples between her fingertips. Her tits felt large and warm and soft as she massaged them. She wanted to touch herself below.

"Yes. Yes." Mark pulled against the cuffs. "I can't stand it." He shut his eyes. He couldn't bear any more. He was going to explode.

Jane wriggled out of her panties and tossed them aside. Her fingers felt for her clit.

"Watch." She didn't even know how the word came out. *Did she really say that?*

Mark's eyes flew open. He licked his lips, desperately wanting to latch onto her rosy clit as she leaned back and rubbed herself. Her face was flushed and alive.

"Watch this." Jane began to feel the hot wave of her climax. She throbbed. She watched Mark writhe in helplessness in the chair. His muscles racked as he pulled and gasped.

"Yes. Oh. Yes." Mark's words were a growl.

Jane felt herself climbing. With her wet fingers she seized his shaft and rubbed. Straddling his legs, she moved his cock head up and down against her clit, pushing his tip hard against hers. Mark began to shake. His taut arms and legs shuddered urgently. He would not be able to hold on much longer.

Jane needed him inside her now. She was ready and she wanted all of him, all of his massive cock, his rod inside her, filling and expanding her until she felt full, felt fulfilled. She flipped around and thrust out her ass, then drove herself down onto his hardness, feeling the heat as he slid up into her. His cock was so thick she felt herself open to him wider and wider. He was farther in than he had ever been. She felt him expanding her, her body greedily accepting his massive thrusting heat. He was all the way in. She looked over her shoulder into his gentle brown eyes. His breath caught. He was on the edge. She pounded down onto him, holding her ground, feeling her own rising pulse as she watched him surrender. His cries filled the air. His body arched and strained as he filled her with hot come.

She stood and faced him. Then she leaned her gorgeous breasts in for his mouth to suck. He sucked and pulled until she came. Then she stood back up, looming proudly over him, naked, exposed, and sure of herself. Mark looked up at his amazing woman, her breasts cutting perfect soft arcs, and her lovely face with the studious glasses.

She released him then. They both were freed that night.

Sasha Channing

I'd fire my whole team and put in a private elevator.

Up and Down

Denise Reardon gazed out her office window to the bustling street below. Absently tapping a perfectly manicured nail against the windowsill, she pondered the lives of those hustling to and fro on the hot pavement. They all seemed so removed from her, part of a life she hadn't experienced in a long time.

Her office suite, located on the penthouse floor, was the envy of everyone in her building, possibly the city. This, coupled with her position, made her one of the most powerful people in the country, man or woman. Being powerful afforded her what she'd always longed for: control.

Lately, however, she found herself becoming bored with this role. It was tedious, provoking fear or jealousy in everyone around her. She could see the ambition and resentment in people's eyes: her assistants and secretaries and doormen . . . and of course, Denise thought with a smile, the delivery boys.

Denise returned to her swivel chair and made a call to the bistro across the street.

"This is Miss Reardon on the twenty-second floor. I'll have my usual," she demanded over the speakerphone. "And if you're late, don't expect a tip." Click!

At precisely one o'clock, there was a forceful knock on the door. "Delivery!"

"Come in," Denise purred.

Antonio opened the door and sauntered to her desk, pausing to give her a thorough once-over. Denise perched on the edge of her desk. She had eschewed her normal buttoned-up look for a somewhat sheer blouse over an obviously expensive and very lacy camisole. Both were tucked loosely into a slim pencil skirt that showed off her shapely legs. Casually, he deposited her order on the desk, then turned to go.

Denise watched him, preparing to pounce. Just before he reached the elevator, she sprang. The cubicle workers gaped as she darted by.

"You forgot part of my delivery," she announced angrily, joining him in the elevator. The doors shut, shielding them from the prying eyes of the world and cocooning them in a private chamber.

Antonio whipped around and hit the Emergency Stop button, then slammed his muscular arms on either side of Denise's body, trapping her.

"This what you want?" he growled softly, dangerously, and reached up her thigh. With deft young fingers he undid her garter and let the soft material slide down her legs. Denise gasped with yearning. The loss of control was intoxicating.

"Yes," she answered quietly.

In the elevator, their roles reversed. The huntress became the prey. The boss became the servant. She existed at his mercy.

"What was that? Speak louder," Antonio snarled, grasping her hair in a bunched fist and forcibly raising her face until their eyes met heatedly.

"Yes, master," she repeated, slightly louder, her face flushed and her pulse quickening. "This is what I want."

She and Antonio had an understanding. For months, every other Thursday they met this way, two bodies crashing and pulsing. For her it was a loss of control, the chance to feel powerless. She longed to connect with someone who could strip her of her artificial traits and bring her life back to a primal, carnal level.

For him it was a rush to dominate the hottest, richest, and most glamorous corporate woman.

Of course the every other Thursday had soon become every Thursday and then that, too, had changed to be almost daily. She knew people had noticed in her office. She knew they were talking, albeit quietly, behind her back about the deliveries she was getting, about how she changed her clothes each day, about her flushed face and tousled hair after her daily ride in the elevator. She knew they talked, but she couldn't stop herself from calling and it seemed he couldn't stop from answering.

She was considering having a private elevator installed just for her with secure access from her office. She was considering firing everyone and hiring all new staff. She was considering a lot of things, but not at this particular moment, not here, in the elevator, not now, in his arms.

Working quickly, Antonio unfastened his Italian leather belt and whipped it out of his jeans. Denise tensed with anticipation, even as she knew what would come next. Moments later, her hands were bound behind her and she'd been shoved facefirst, into the elevator wall.

"Ohh!" she cooed helplessly, loving every second.

Antonio bit the nape of her neck and bunched her skirt up for easier access. Her soft, bare flesh welcomed his wandering hands. Alternating between gentle and rough caresses, he manipulated her body without shame. When neither of them could take any more, he stepped out of his pants and positioned himself at her swollen entrance from behind. A few shallow thrusts and then he was buried to the hilt, pushing in and out, up and down.

She cried out, gyrating against him until he took charge and held her tightly, making her stay still.

"Be quiet," he ordered crossly, but she couldn't obey; the pleasure was too deep. He smacked her firmly across the ass and her inner walls squeezed around him, deliciously tight. Suddenly, she felt him yank her bound wrists up with one hand. The other snaked around her neck to cover her mouth.

"I said, be quiet!"

She nodded frantically, voice muffled, just hoping he would continue thrusting inside her.

He didn't disappoint. The pace quickened, and he rode her to completion, slumping against her back with relief and exhaustion. Frustrated, she whimpered into his now-slack hand. *What about me?*

"If you want release, you're going to have to beg," he muttered into her damp hair.

Denise tried to turn in his arms and he allowed it, removing his hand from her lips so she could plead with him properly.

"Please, please, oh, please," she whispered, her entire body shaking with desire.

"Get on your knees," Antonio responded and she obeyed without hesitation.

Slowly she kissed a trail up his leg, pausing to inhale his musky scent blended with the salty sweet smell of her own juices. Amazingly, he was growing hard again. Denise took him in her mouth and gently sucked. As her excitement built he stopped her, hauling her body up his and fitting back inside her. Bracing her against the elevator doors, he took her repeatedly, this time using his hand to massage her between the legs and bring her to an earth-shattering climax. They clung together for a few seconds, breathing hard, then simultaneously pulled apart and straightened their clothing.

Antonio pushed the down button and exited to the street. Denise pressed the penthouse button and traveled back up to the sky.

On her desk, untouched, sat Antonio's delivery. Denise opened it with shaking fingers, her body and skin still tingling from their fevered coupling. Inside was a note: "Drinks tonight?—A."

She grinned. Drinks after work gave her something entirely new to consider indeed.

Katherine Jay

JennaTip #2: Getting It Up When Going Up

Elevator sex: the ups and downs of connubial bliss in a lift. For an example on film that's R-rated, see *Class* in which Andrew McCarthy and Jacqueline Bisset do the nasty in a glass elevator. This is *not* recommended unless you like the idea of being watched, caught, and prosecuted. What is recommended is that you plan ahead and scope out a likely elevator in a likely building without a lot of security and without a lot of security cameras.

Some more detailed advice on elevator sex is to try using the service elevator because it's less likely to be busy, it's got a stop button that probably doesn't have an alarm attached to it, it may have padded walls, there might be a cart or table in it to lean against or sit on, and that musty dusty smell is always such a turn-on, at least for some people.

If the service elevator is out of the question, then try to find an older elevator with a stop button that does not set off the alarm. You don't want to be rescued by security while in flagrante delicto.

Choose a time that isn't elevator rush hour and you are less likely to be discovered, but keep in mind that there's no real way to be sure you'll get away with it unless you're having elevator sex in your own private elevator, which takes away some of the fun and all of the challenge—unless the challenge is to convince your partner to try it out, in which case that's a whole different pot calling the kettle of fish to fry, or something like that.

Anniversary Surprise

I picked my husband up at the airport on a Friday evening. He had been gone a couple of days on business. It was our wedding anniversary and we were going straight from the airport out.

"How about going to Smitty's first?" I suggested, picking a cool pub with a private room in back with a pool table no one ever seemed to remember was there. We'd have lots of privacy, I knew.

"Really, sweetie? You don't want something fancier?" he asked.

"Naah. I love playing pool with you, you know that."

When we got there, it was just as I thought. The back room was completely quiet. It would be just the two of us.

"I'll get some change and order beers. Be right back." I smacked him on the ass as I went through the narrow corridor leading to the main bar.

When I returned to the back room, my husband had put a box of Godiva chocolates on the table.

"Thanks, baby." I, relinquishing my membership in the great sorority of womanhood, am not a big chocolate eater. He knows this. I figured he wanted to get me something, and he was stuck at an airport all day or on a plane and so had done the best he could. I couldn't blame a guy for trying.

I gave him a big wet kiss, pressing myself up against him, but I didn't open the chocolates. We hadn't eaten dinner yet, had two beers going, and I was ready to rack up the balls for our game.

"Aren't you going to open those?" He was trying to sound patient.

"I'll wait 'til after dinner." I figured he wanted some chocolate. He adores chocolate.

"Please. Open them now."

"Okay, but you probably bought yourself some when you got me these and already ate them, so I don't see why you can't wait." I shouldn't chastise him on our anniversary, but he knows I don't even like chocolate.

I opened the box and found it only half full. The other half had a different box in it with a little white bow pressed to the top. I looked up at my husband, tilting my head to the side with a quizzical look on my face. He just smiled at me.

I picked up the little box and shook it a little. No sound emerged. He smiled a little more. I started to carefully unwrap the paper, trying not to tear it.

"Oh, for God's sake. Just tear the paper, we're going to throw it away anyway." He was really losing his patience. I was intrigued and I do so love the anticipation of surprises.

Once it was unwrapped, I slowly opened it to find a delicate sapphire-and-diamond pendant necklace nestled in tissue. I was so surprised, I didn't know what to say, which is completely unheard of in my case.

I slipped the chain around my neck and then ran off to the bathroom to get a good look. It was just lovely and nestled delicately in my cleavage.

"What made you get this? We cannot afford this. I love it. You spoil me." I babbled on, thrilled and overwhelmed. I wrapped my whole body around him for an even bigger, wetter kiss. I nibbled on his lips and ran my tongue along his teeth. My hands slid down his back and cupped his ass. I pressed against him, kissing him long and hard, rubbing up against his crotch. My left hand came around to the front where I ran my nails along his chest, giving a little extra attention to his nipple area. That little nub sprang to attention. I nipped his jawline, then ran my tongue along his neck, blowing and licking until I sucked at that little hollow spot at his shoulder and neck.

"You're welcome. Step back. Let me see." He was getting aroused and I could feel his cock stirring against me.

"You can look at it later. I'm busy thanking you right now."

He pulled me harder to him then and whispered in my ear, "I missed you so much. I hate being away from you for an hour, much less a few days. You make me so hot. I want you all the time. Tonight, I'm going to make love to you and then I'm going to fuck you all night."

I hadn't eaten much and had gulped down my beer so that it went a little to my head, along with the oxygen deprivation from the deep kisses and heavy breathing. I got a smile on my face that my husband knows only too well. It's my "I am going to do something shockingly naughty to you" smile.

He was sitting on a high bar chair with me caught between his thighs. I took his hand and guided it up under my shirt, encouraging him to cup my breast as I ran my hands up and down along his thighs, kneading his muscles and grabbing at his hips with my fingers while my thumbs rubbed on either side of his now fully erect penis.

"What in the world . . ." He was breathing quickly.

"Shhhh. Now, it's my turn to surprise you." I was just about to pounce when I realized the waitress was coming. We tried to turn our heavy petting into a more platonic hug, only to burst out laughing and giggling, with me turning scarlet from my chest up my neck and ears and into my hairline. Curse my Scottish skin.

"Can I get you anything? Sorry I've taken so long. I didn't know anyone was here." She smiled at us.

"A couple more beers and some chicken nachos would be great," my husband said as he tried to surreptitiously adjust himself.

"Anything else you need?" She had to know something was up, and looking down I could see it was still way up. No wonder he was squirming.

"Nope. We're perfect." I grinned at her.

After she walked back out of the room, we took a breather and drank a bit more beer. This just loosened me up and it wasn't long before I was rubbing up against him again, tickling his neck, and cupping his now-semihard penis through his pants.

"She'll be right back." He hissed into my hair.

"Do you want me to stop?"

"Yes. No. Ahh hell." He stopped struggling, scooped me up, kissing me until I thought I'd pass out.

We broke apart again as she set down the beer and food. She looked at us, smiled, and said, "If that's it for you, I'll leave you alone for a bit."

"Yup. Great. Got everything. Thanks." We chorused to her back as she had already turned to leave.

"God, you're obvious," he said. He clearly didn't realize his shirt was gaping open where I'd popped a button off or that he had a smear of red lipstick from his cheek down his neck.

Ignoring our food and drink, I undid his belt, popped open his jeans button, and lowered the zipper to provide some air to his throbbing cock.

"Let's talk about obvious, shall we?" I stared at his bulging boxers. Slipping my fingers into his boxer fly, I eased out his rock-hard dick. I ran the tip of my finger along the slit and rubbed the pre-come around the purple head.

"Mmmm." He sighed and adjusted his hips a bit to provide more play space. I pressed the boxers back around his cock and started to stroke him as I kissed him deeply and he grabbed and released my hips and ass. After just a short time of this, I smiled that smile again and quickly dipped my head down to kiss the top of his cock, running my tongue along the edge, flicking at that spot right where the head meets the shaft. His cock danced in response, spontaneously jerking a little, and a soft moan escaped from his lips.

"Look at what you do to me." He could barely form words.

Taking him quickly into my mouth, running my hand down his shaft, I quickly followed with my mouth.

"You love it when I do this." I mumbled around the cock-head in my mouth.

"Oh, yes. You're driving me crazy."

"Want me to stop?" I asked again.

"Good lord, no. I'd die." I played with his head with my tongue.

"I am so going to fuck you when we get home. I am going to lean you over and fuck you on all fours, flip you around, and make you meow like a cat." I was getting really hot listening to him.

"Promise?"

"Twice."

I could feel that little knot form at the base of his penis, the one that lets me know he is getting really close. I felt his cock go rigid in my mouth. I caressed him as he came.

"Let's put that monster away before someone gets hurt," I purred as I helped slip his still-hard cock back into his pants.

Not a moment too soon, as the waitress came round the corner to see how we were doing. She saw the untouched and now quite cold nachos, the unplayed game of pool, and the two of us with wide, idiotic grins plastered across our faces.

"You look like you're doing fine. Want me to reheat those nachos for you?" She had to know, but she was being really cool.

"Pack 'em up to go." My husband almost growled at her as he wrapped his arm about me, pressing his still-massive cock into the small of my back. "We've got a hungry beast to feed once we get home."

Adina Giordano

What a fantastic fantasy of a kick-ass hottie I'd love to meet and greet in a crowded LA bar.

Spellbound

Walking up to me at the bar in Los Angeles, this fantasy with wild dark hair, ass-kickin' heels leading up to round hips and a curvy ass, and lovely breasts tossing about in a deep V-cut silk top opened her luscious mouth and said, "I don't really see what all the fuss over you is about, you're not as hot as all my friends seem to think you are."

As she talked, she twisted a strand of that long, dark hair around her finger. If this was her idea of a pickup, it was working like a charm.

"I mean you have a nice body, your arms look defined, your jaw is strong, and your eyes are really a piercing blue, but I've just never been one to fall for a guy who looks like he should model when he isn't splitting wood at his very expensive ski-in and -out chalet." She ran a finger down my merino wool sweater, along my arm, and ended by tapping a well-shaped fingernail on my Cartier as she said all this. All I really heard was "in and out," though I hung on her every word—or at least appeared to—as I imagined tasting her wet candy-colored lips.

"But, I told my friends . . . see them over there?" she pointed back to a group of hot sexy women all staring at us, "I told them I would give you the benefit of the doubt and, after you buy me a drink, I'll let you wow me with you sparkling conversation, proving them right and me wrong."

"Pardon?" was all I managed, but at least it sounded more cultured than "hunh?"

There went wowing her with sparkling conversation.

"A dirty martini," she responded.

Then she turned me around, physically, and pushed me toward the bar with a little finger wave and a pointed look at her own watch.

You may be wondering what I did. If you are, then you haven't been paying attention. I went and bought her a dirty martini. What else was I supposed to do?

Intense and possibly a little crazy, she was also so incredibly sexy and clearly aggressive, intelligent, and not afraid to go get what she wants. It is very difficult to find that combination. It is nearly impossible to do so in a bar. It is a billion times a billion to one to do so in a bar in Los Angeles. Yet, here she was.

There was no way I was going to let this opportunity slip away. I asked the bartender for a shot of something to clear my head. He asked me what I had in mind. I pointed to the woman, the mirage, the dream that was waiting for me, tapping her toes with impatience, and he nodded. I don't know what it was he gave me, it was on fire, made my eyes water and nose run, cleared up my sinuses, made my hair tingle, and almost knocked me off my feet. Asking for a beer chaser, I got her a dirty martini and walked back to where she stood. In that wild, hectic bar crowd, she was like an oasis. People parted to make way for me as I walked back to her, pulled as I was into her orbit.

Up close, I could see that her eyes were a muddy green, that her hair had streaks of light mixed in with the velvety blackness of it, and that she was wearing a lace and silk camisole under her top, which allowed her lovely breasts to sway freely with hard nipples poking through and daring me to stare.

She rolled her eyes at the music and at the crowd, then suggested that I should find a quiet table for us. The place was packed and I didn't think there was any possibility of my finding a table, but the look on her face and the way her body vibrated just standing there made it clear I should do my damnedest.

I went to the quietest corner in the place and bought the table from the guy and girl sitting there. The girl was pissed, but clearly he felt that my $100 bill was worth more to him than her happiness that evening.

I escorted this bewitching beauty to the table, pulled out her chair for her before sitting down myself, holding my breath to see what next impossible task she would set in my way.

She took a sip, licked those incredible lips again, and then just sat there, watching me and obviously waiting.

She made me really nervous and I was having a tough time thinking at all around her. Finally, it dawned on me that I was meant to wow her with my conversation and that if I didn't begin soon, I'd be sitting at my $100 table all alone kicking the shit out of myself.

So, I began. In French. See, I'm from Southern France, and my family owns a winery or two. I live part of the time in France and part of the time wherever I feel, and at the moment, I was feeling like living in Southern California. I was actually doing some work, checking out the California wine areas, and had decided to enjoy a little bit of Hollywood while I was on the West Coast. Since I wasn't able to think straight and have an intelligent and witty conversation in English, what with all the blood in my body having abandoned my brain, I resorted to French. It wasn't particularly witty, but I was hoping she didn't speak the language and would just fall for the whole foreign thing.

She had, of course, lived in Paris for four years as a fashion designer and was fluent.

I thought I was screwed, but I guess I had impressed her simply by being able to understand her, follow her directions, and

speak more than one language, even if the gist of what I was saying wasn't particularly inspired.

After that evening and every evening of my two-week stay in
Los Angeles, we discovered more in common than the pure, animal physical attraction we felt. I am not only always hot for her
body, I am absolutely hot for her brain, and she's coming with
me to my family estate to meet my parents.

I don't know what was in the shot I drank, but I think it was
a love potion, because I'm totally spellbound.

Genevieve Noelle

JennaTip #3: Love Potions

I don't know if there really are any love potions out there, but others have done research into aphrodisiacs and the science behind the story.

The following is a brief collection of items, though I really don't think any would make a very good drink. Except maybe for the oyster. Raw-oyster shooters are quite popular and just might do the trick.

Oysters are a shellfish rich in zinc, a mineral your body needs for the production of testosterone, the hormone that is behind the male sex drive and is also associated with the female libido. Shuck them. Suck them. Eat them raw!

Chocolate contains a stimulant that has been shown to give people a feeling of excitement and well-being not unlike the way endorphins work in the body. Plus, it tastes so good.

Asparagus is shaped like a penis and has a lot of vitamin E, which stimulates the production of sex hormones. If you can get around the smell of your pee, a well known side effect of eating asparagus, then by all means put a sprig of asparagus in your Bloody Mary and see where it gets you.

Spanish fly is one of the most notorious of love potions, but it is illegal in the United States. The reason it seems to work is because it sends a rush of blood to the genitals and irritates the urinary tract, but it can cause infections and scarring and death, and on top of that it's made from the dried body of a beetle, which is kind of gross, all in all.

Oyster Shooter Recipe:
A fat, juicy raw oyster

A splash of cocktail sauce (tomato sauce, horseradish, pepper)

A squeeze of lemon

A full jigger of vodka

Five thousand, two hundred and eighty feet, a just barely
big enough blanket, a few vodka tonics, and I'm there, baby.

LAX-Rated

She always puts her keys in the same place when she gets home, so why is she, as the airport limo waits outside, frantically rummaging through her apartment looking for them? Running twenty minutes late, having finally located them on the floor of the bathroom next to the third outfit she's put on and taken off, Caroline is finally out the door. *Why is she so concerned about her appearance just to fly from LAX to JFK to see family?* She finally opted for the skirt because her black leather boots wouldn't fit in her luggage and she had bought the boots especially for New York and they looked killer with the skirt, though also nice with her jeans, but her jeans were at the bottom of the suitcase and the skirt in the middle.

Arriving at LAX, the usual airport chaos further unnerves her. Making her way through families saying tearful good-byes or hopeful hellos, she joins the zombies in the snaking coffee line. No way will she board the plane without caffeine and a trashy tabloid to read. She isn't a fan of flying and now that the flight attendants are as likely to toss you off the plane for asking for a pillow as help you find one, she needs all the comfort items she can manage to locate once through security.

Caroline no sooner sits down to catch her breath and look at the photos of which drugged-up former child star was losing custody of her precious and sadly ignored little ones in La-La Land, when the loudspeaker announces they are: "Now boarding rows number 35 through 25."

"Damn, not even enough time to read the captions," she fumes. Quickly gathering her stuff, she gets into yet another line. While waiting, she scans the people around her, noticing a very attractive man three people behind. Just then, he looks up and their eyes meet.

"Wow! Big and blue." Her immediate reaction is followed quickly by a glance downward, at which point she finds herself thinking "Wow! Big."

Caroline is not normally so horny, but, jeez, this guy sets her blood pumping.

Realizing she's staring, she drops her eyes in embarrassment.

Settling into her aisle seat, she crosses her fingers the row will stay empty. Then big and blue appears. He settles into the seat next to her, giving her a closer look.

Strong jaw, full lips, and, God, what is the fabulous smell? She chastises herself for being so naughty, then inhales deeply again.

Amazingly, the plane takes off on time and soon the flight attendant is making the rounds with the beverage cart.

"I could use a drink. I really hate flying." He turns to her.

Caroline smiles encouragingly.

"My name is Dan." A well-shaped forearm extends, and her hand disappears in his larger one.

"Caroline." She realizes she is still holding on to his hand. "Um, I hate flying, too."

Caroline orders a vodka tonic for her nerves, though she never drinks on flights. Dan certainly unsettles her. He orders the same.

With each drink, the conversation moves from the inane to the more personal, and the friendly touching lasts longer and grows more intense. The lights dim on the plane and people all around close their shades for the movie.

"Can we get some blankets here?" Dan asks the passing flight attendant. "It's a bit chilly."

Shocked that he isn't hog-tied and put in the overhead bin for his effrontery, Caroline realizes that his smile works on other women, too, as a thorough search is made on his behalf by not just one but three flight attendants. Only one blanket is found, so Dan covers both their laps with it. Then, leaning in close, he whispers, "I think you're beautiful."

As Caroline is leaning in to say "thank you," the plane hits some turbulence, smashing their lips together. Dan pulls back a little, but Caroline keeps right with him.

God, what's gotten into me? she wonders as she kisses him harder.

Once he realizes she isn't offended by the accidental kiss, far from it, he leans back in, slipping his tongue between her lips and teeth. He tastes as yummy as he smells.

Next, his soft full lips brush her upper lip, then lower. His hand slips behind her neck as he grabs the back of her hair.

Forgetting entirely about the hundreds of other passengers as his tongue caresses her, Caroline feels as though they are completely alone.

With each teasing kiss and tongue stroke, she wants him more. She is definitely getting hotter than she'd ever been in a plane, and it isn't because of the blanket.

His kisses unbelievably grow harder and last longer. Grabbing the blanket folded neatly over their knees, he opens it to full size, draping both their bodies. His hand touches the outside of her thigh. As he rubs her leg, her knees open, allowing his hand to slide up her thigh and under her skirt.

As he kisses her neck, her breathing becomes heavy. Again, their lips meet, and Caroline feels her panties growing soaked.

Suddenly, she wants him to know. Taking his hand, she leads it farther up her thigh until he slips a finger under the lacy edge of her panties. He readily slips a finger between her swollen lips, finding her pulsing clit, and runs his fingertip over it before moving his finger lower and sliding it up inside her. Holding his hand, Caroline slowly moves it back and forth. Releasing him as he gets the hang of what she wants, she sets her own hand free to wander.

Beginning at his smooth chest, Caroline unbuttons his shirt, then runs her nails along his well-defined abs. In one deft move, she pulls his belt loose. His hard cock is straining against his jeans. Unzipping him, she caresses the helmet and the shaft.

As she rubs slowly and rhythmically, he plunges his finger deeper inside. Then he has two in, two large and thick fingers. He goes slowly. Once inside, he begins pushing. Pushing hard at first, then harder.

As Caroline strokes him, his breathing deepens and his excitement gets her more excited. His pace quickens. With her legs now open as wide as the blanket permits, she hikes up her skirt and pushes her wet panties farther to the side.

"Not yet," he moans quietly.

Oh God, she is close and getting closer, her legs uncontrollably shaking. Dan takes a sharp breath and groans as he comes.

For the remainder of the flight they kiss and fondle one another, then try to surreptitiously put themselves back together. He helps her get her things together, but disappears almost immediately upon deplaning. Caroline is a little disappointed, but also relieved as she sees her mom, dad, and younger brother waiting for her.

When her trip to New York ends, Caroline is totally bemused

to find she's been upgraded to first class for the return trip. After settling into her seat and getting her requested blanket, she looks up to see sparkling wine and behind the wine, sparkling blue eyes.

Sherrie Curtis

JennaTip #4: 5,280 Feet High

We are not talking about having sex in Denver, the mile-high city. Nope. This is about having sex in an airplane, something that once upon a time was very popular and not so hard to pull off, especially since rumor has it the flight attendants were more than willing to help out. Of course, that was before 9/11 and the crackdown on terrorists slipping into the small bathrooms of the planes to get a little nookie.

Now, the safest way to join the club is to pay around $400 for a one-to-two-hour flight in a private plane where the pilot circles the area, provides champagne, mood music, and instead of seats, there is a mattress in the back.

Sure it's safer and you won't go to jail or be fined some outrageous amount of money for imperiling the security of our country by having a quickie in the john, but it also is cheating and really should not count.

You can try to join by having sex under a blanket, but since people have been told they aren't allowed on a flight for wearing a short skirt and V-neck top because it is too risqué, it might just be time to retire the mile-high-club membership requirements and just let people go to Denver for a quickie.

Sweat, sex, and a couple gallons of paint sounds like a good time.

Company Party

She rubbed her forehead. "But you have to come. It's your company party."

"Sweetie, if I can get this deal wrapped up quickly, I might make it, but not if you don't let me leave. It's a five million dollar account. I can't afford to leave anything to chance."

"James, they'll understand! Just—"

His own frustration became evident. "Give me a break, will you? If something goes wrong, they will *not* understand. If that happens, you can say good-bye to your new car, your big home, to everything."

"They're just things. I don't need them. I need you."

"Look around you, Leah. You've got your own studio, expensive art to hang on the walls, anything you want. Do you really want to give it all up?"

Before she could answer, he shrugged on his suit jacket. Checking his watch, he gave her an absent peck on the cheek. "I promise I'll try to make the party and make it up to you." And then he was out the door. Leah sank down on the bed.

It was a lovely home, certainly. But he was wrong when he said she had anything she wanted. She wanted him, and he was unavailable.

She had recently been longing for the cramped, water-stained one-room apartment they first shared. They had been young. They had been in love. It had been heaven. They had made love every night back then, before he was too busy. She'd hop up afterward and, naked, paint murals on the walls while he stayed in bed, watching.

The phone rang.

"Are you two ready?" It was Alexis, James's partner's wife. She was a brassy blonde with whom Leah had struck up an unlikely friendship.

"Rick's still swearing at his cummerbund," Alexis continued. "He says formal events always remind him of his prom."

Leah, attempting humor, "If he gives you a wilted pink carnation, just smile and say thank you."

"Cute. We'll pick you up around eight. Does that work?"

"James can't make it. I think I'll cancel."

"What?"

"He's working."

"It's his party!"

"I know. But, there's not much I can do, is there?"

Leah heard Alexis call out to her husband, "Why is James going into the office? He's going to miss the party!"

Rick's muffled response sounded a lot like "Lucky bastard" to Leah.

Alexis came back on the line. "So. You'll go stag."

"I really think I'll just pass, Lexi. I'll call you Saturday, maybe we can do brunch—"

"You're going. I said so. No arguments." Her voice turned cajoling. "You have a dress, right?"

Leah looked down. She did have a dress, a very sexy, very slinky, very red dress. It was gorgeous.

If she skipped the party, she'd end up on the couch eating ice cream and watching *The English Patient,* the dress back in the closet.

"You win. Pick me up at eight. I'll be ready."

Two hours later, she was standing next to the punch bowl alone in her sexy red dress.

Lexi and Rick were dancing. Lexi caught her eye and waved enthusiastically. Leah waved back. When they turned away, she frowned, wishing the evening would be over already.

A large hand gripped her elbow suddenly.

"Don't tell me," James whispered into her neck, "that some fool stood you up."

"It's not like it's the first time." Before the words were out of her mouth she winced. "What I mean is—"

"Shh."

His hand was still on her elbow, and she realized he was subtly guiding her across the room, toward the terrace and the dark lawn beyond.

"Where are we going?"

"I promised I'd make it up to you when I got here."

Outside, the air was cool. Torches lined the path but she still had difficulty seeing. She faltered.

James caught her in a strong grip. "Careful, beautiful. Wouldn't want to tear that dress." He bent down and nipped her neck, then whispered "At least not yet."

Ahead she glimpsed a gazebo, silent and shuttered. James stepped in front of her and gave the door a kick. It swung open easily and he pulled her inside.

Her eyes hadn't adjusted to the darkness. "James?"

He ripped the dress from her body.

She stood there in strappy heels and panties. His breath was hot in her ear. "No bra? Good."

"My God, James . . . the dress—" Speech failed her as his hands found her breasts. He was demanding and powerful. She arched into his touch.

He pulled her down to the floor. Blankets had already been spread beneath them. She looked around, thinking that the gazebo was about the size of that first little apartment.

He nudged her legs apart, knelt between them. He fingered the wet silk that covered her crotch. "I want to taste you."

She was breathless, not able to say a word.

He stripped her completely. For a moment she lay bare and exposed, the cool air tickling her. Then he bent down and his tongue parted her lips.

She bucked. He braced his hands on her thighs and held her steady.

"Where do you think you're going?" And he returned to his task.

Long, deep, thorough licks ignited her. She called out to him, nonsense, wordless moans. He was ruthless. Pushing her to the edge.

"Please," she begged. "Please, please, please . . ."

His tongue circled her. She strained upward, fist clenched, head thrown back.

He kissed her. "You're delicious. A man could live on that." He was straddling her hips, and his hardness nudged at her.

"I'm going to take you, right here on the floor."

She knew she should be worried about being discovered, but the idea just ratcheted her arousal up another notch.

Without warning, he entered her. She was soaking wet and ready.

"You were waiting for me, weren't you?"

She nodded, not trusting her voice. He pulled out, almost all the way, and then rammed forward again. Deeper. Harder.

"Well," he said. "I'm home now."

She imagined the sight: James, mounted above her, naked.

His muscled back shining with sweat, her fingers digging into his arms.

He drove into her fiercely. He spread one hand across her chest, over her heart. "You're so close," he murmured. "I can always tell. Come with me, Leah." Their gazes locked.

In response she wrapped her legs around him, bringing him impossibly closer. She bit his nipple, then kissed along his neck and jaw.

That seemed to break something within him. His thrusts became frenzied and his frantic pace sent her over the edge. She cried out, not caring who might be listening.

Just before he came inside her, he dropped his forehead to hers. "There are paint cans in the corner. We have all night."

Cheri Lawson

Rushing Roulette

My best friend forever, Bethany, and I were going through sorority rush at our big Southern school. We knew we would go to the same house, we absolutely had to, because Bethany and I have a really special relationship where we share everything, and I mean everything, and so if we went to different houses, then we would have to keep the sorority secrets from each other, and we'd never be able to do that.

Anyway, Bethany and I have known each other for about ten years, ever since she moved onto my family's block and we started riding the bus to school together. We hit puberty together, comparing our breasts, hips, asses, and the hair growth on our trim little twats. She did a bikini wax on me when I was too embarrassed to go get it done in a salon. She left her pussy hairy, though. She liked the way the hair got all wet and she could pull at it when she was horny. I liked it, too, on her.

So, we were high school cheerleaders together, went to cheerleader camp, which let me tell you something, really is about smoking pot, drinking too much, fooling around, and a little bit about "skill" building. I assure you, the pyramids we did in the rooms were a hell of a lot more to cheer about than anything we did at the games.

Anyway, we decided to go through rush together. We also had made the cheer squad for the school, so we were a pretty hot commodity. At a big football school, being a cheerleader and having access to the team for dating and parties is a really big deal. Some of these guys are going to go pro and make lots of money and be on TV.

We were at a big away game and had beaten the bejesus out of the rival loser team and Bethany and I were celebrating with a bunch of people who had made the trip. It was mostly a group of girls from our rush group, you know the girls you go to all the houses with in teams.

Even though we were the away team, the local bars and clubs had tons of specials for us to celebrate our victory and we were doing Jaeger shots and flaming something or other shots and getting really loose and crazy. It was hotter than hell since it was early September and the club was packed and Bethany and I were all wet and sweaty. We also kept rubbing up against each other and everyone else because there just wasn't any room to breathe at all.

I was so horny from all the bodies rubbing against me and the drink and everything that I grabbed Bethany by the hand and dragged her to the bathroom. The line for the girls' room went all the way around the bar, so, yelling that it was an emergency, we skipped the line and went into the guys' bathroom.

What is it with these stupid bars that they have room capacity for five hundred people, but then have one fucking stall per bathroom? Normally I get really p.o.'d about this kind of thing, but this time I was all for it because it meant that Bethany and I could lock the door and have a little space and privacy.

I flipped my long blond hair over and started throwing handfuls of cold tap water on my neck to cool down as Bethany leaned against the bathroom wall watching me. She was clearly as hot as I was, because you could see the outline of her C-cup breasts through her shirt where the sweat below and between them had soaked the cotton. She had on a pleated little miniskirt and no stockings. No panties, either, as I soon found out. I looked up from the sink to watch her in the mirror, smiling at her and shaking my ass back and forth as I ran my cool, wet hands down my neck and along my chest. I was in a tiny little tank top that dipped well down into my cleavage. I'm not as big as Bethany, with just B-cups, but this top showed them off to their very best advantage.

Bethany was obviously enjoying the view she was getting. She lifted the hem of her skirt, exposing her hairy snatch, and started to finger her clit with one hand as she smoked her cigarette with the other. It was such a hot and dirty look I almost creamed watching her. I turned around and put my little ass up on the sink. The cool porcelain felt great on my hot cheeks and thighs. I leaned back against the mirror and sat there looking at Bethany as I started to massage my breasts and pinch my nipples.

She put out her cigarette and then sauntered over to where I was perched. She ran her hand up underneath my mane of hair, pulled me close to her, and gave me a smoky, alcoholic kiss, sliding her tongue in my mouth and then sucking on my lips. She's always been the dom in our relationship, running the show and having her way, every way. I whimpered into her mouth because I wanted her so much. She ran her tongue down my chin and neck, pushed aside the thin little strap of my top and latched onto my hard rosy brown nipple. She sucked and licked and bit and kissed my breast and nipple until I came, right there on the sink. She slid her hand up under my skirt and pushed aside the filmy little bit of fabric I was wearing and pushed first one and then a second finger up inside me. She twisted her hand around so she could hit my G-spot and started tapping away at it as she kept licking my breasts and neck. I was thrashing around moaning and when I came this time, I wet her whole hand with my juicy come.

Right about this time there was a really loud knocking on the door and we could suddenly hear a lot of screaming and hollering from the other side. I guess we'd been in that bathroom for at least ten minutes. I tried to hop down off the sink, but Bethany made me stay right where I was. She asked me if I was interested in playing a little game. I said "Sure, what?" She said how about a little roulette? I asked her what she meant and she said she would open the door, grab the first person she could get her hands on from the other side, drag them into the bathroom with us, and we would fuck them, male or female, right then and there.

My mouth dropped open and all I could do was nod my agreement. Bethany threw the door open, reached out and grabbed someone's arm, pulled them in, turned the light off at the same time, and then slammed the door shut and locked it.

At first, all I could hear was some startled heavy breathing. Then a big, gruff voice asked what the hell was going on.

Oh, goody! A man. I really do love me some hard dick and was aching to be filled up with one following the fabulous finger-fucking I'd just gotten from Bethany. She'd just as well preferred another girl, but she'd just make do.

I guess Bethany grabbed the guy by the nuts, because I heard a yelp and then a sigh as she started caressing him a bit more gently. She must have guided his hands up to her big titties, because he started to say something about liking the feel of them when she covered his mouth with her other hand and then guided him over to where I was on the sink. She moved one of his hands off her tits and put it on mine. I don't know what must have been going through his mind, but based on my experience with men, he probably wasn't doing a whole lot of thinking right about then.

He pulled and grabbed at my breasts as Bethany unzipped his pants and pulled out his whopper of a cock. I heard her gasp and he chuckled, clearly impressed with himself. Bethany grabbed him by the hips and turned him so he was facing me and helped guide that great big dick up inside of me. He latched on to my hips and thighs with his huge hands and pulled me onto him so my ass was barely resting on the edge of the sink and proceeded to fuck me long and hard. Bethany's a bit of a bitch sometimes and I guess she thought she wasn't having nearly as much fun now as I was, so she set about to surprise this good ole boy a little more—she sunk her thumb up in his ass as he was driving his rod into me.

He hollered a little and then came good and hard, collapsing a little onto me as I clung to the sink to keep from falling off. It was a little fast but still felt so good to be totally filled up with his hot cock.

Still in the dark, he reached around me, turned on the water and washed his hands, then stumbled out the door, which Bethany quickly locked again. She turned the light on and looked at me, all sweaty and disheveled, sitting up against the mirror, and asked if I was game for a few more rounds. I said was she fucking kidding me. I was up for an all-night spin of rushing roulette if she was.

Genevieve Noelle

Walk hard and carry a big dick, now that's my idea of law enforcement.

Police Story

I really couldn't believe it when it happened. It was like my fantasies, but wilder. My heart pumped so hard, as hard as my hand on his cock, I thought I would pass out. Well, let me slow down a little and start somewhere closer to the beginning.

It was a sunny, warm, gorgeous day, the kind of day where you call in sick and play hooky, which is exactly what I did. I wasn't lying, either. I was sick. Sick and tired of going to my drab cubicle and working all day under fluorescent lighting that made my skin look green.

So, there I was, top down on my candy blue Mini convertible with the white racing stripes, rockin' out to the flashback 80s tunes playing on the radio, winding my way along a mostly deserted road when I heard the siren. It actually took me awhile to hear the siren, since the music was turned up so loud, but when the song ended, there it was, blaring away. I looked in the rearview mirror and sure enough, motorcycle cop, right behind me, waving me over to the side of the road.

Damn, but that sure did put a cloud in my blue-skies day. I put on my signal and slowed down. There wasn't much choice for where to pull over as the road was in the hills, but I finally found a gravel clearing.

Well, he sat for a bit on his bike, just kind of staring at me through his mirrored sunglasses. I was getting nervous with him not getting off the bike and coming to get my license and registration and asking me if I knew why he'd pulled me over and all that typical cop stuff. Then, from the other direction, another motorcycle cop appeared. This one pulled over next to "my" cop. They spoke briefly together, then "my" cop finally got off his bike and came to the window.

"License and registration, please."

"Of course, officer. Must be nice riding that bike on beautiful days like today." I was trying hard to be friendly and helpful, but didn't seem to be getting anywhere.

"Do you know . . ."

". . . why you pulled me over?" I interrupted him. "Why no, I can't say that I do. I wasn't speeding and my taillights are all working." I was really trying hard to be charming. I batted my eyes a bit. He was a tall, cool drink of water in his uniform, which clung in all the right spots and bulged in all the right spots, too.

He gave me a tight grin, not showing much humor, and said he'd be back.

"Shit," I thought. "Why did he pull me over?" I really hadn't been going much over the speed limit, hardly enough over to justify a ticket. Maybe I'd just get a warning.

I watched him in my mirror. He was talking to the other cop. He handed that cop my license. I don't think I look like a criminal or fugitive and I just couldn't figure out what was going on when the other cop got off the bike and walked up to the side of my car. As soon as *she* got off the bike, I figured out that *she* was a *she*. Her clinging uniform bulged in strategic spots making me think of the dangerous curves signs I'd seen a few miles earlier.

She asked me to step out of the car. Now, I was getting worried.

"What seems to be the problem, officer?" I asked. *She* just asked me again to "step out of the car."

What else could I do? I stepped out. She asked me to turn around and put my hands on the hood of my little Mini. I was really confused and didn't know what to think, so I did as she asked. The Mini is a mighty low car. I had to really lean down to get my hands on it. She had me spread my legs. I was trembling a little. She took her baton off her belt and started to slide it down the outside of my legs. I don't know what she was looking for, especially since I had on a short, flirty little skirt and my legs were bare. Then she ran the baton up the inside of my legs and up under the skirt to rest against my mound. I started to squirm and was about to turn around when she pressed up against me with her healthy chest pushing into my back and the baton angling up so that the tip was pressing my pussy lips right where my clit is. I couldn't move and was off balance. She whispered in my ear that she was going to have to do a full-body search and that I'd best just relax.

By this time, her partner cop had come up and he was standing on the other side of my car. Because of the angle, he had a perfect view down my V-neck and could see my creamy white breasts as they dangled and hung there, swaying slightly.

While I was watching him looking down my shirt, I noticed that his bulges were bulging a hell of a lot more. The female cop flipped my skirt up, exposing my cheeks, split by a bit of red thong. She invited her partner to come over and "assist" her in her search.

I know I should have made a scene, but, God, was I turned on and he was so hot and I just found myself going along.

He came around to the driver's side and stepped immediately behind me. She removed her baton and I thought he was using it when I realized that it wasn't a baton that was rubbing up and along my crease. The cool breeze tingled along the damp line he drew with his clearly excited cock. His pre-come was leaving a trail as he pressed and glided his cockhead along my ass.

As he continued to push and rub against me, she slid her hands up under my loose top, rubbing them lightly along my ribs to just beneath my breasts. Suddenly, she grabbed and cupped me, pulling at my hard nipples through my lacy silk bra cups. I let out a mew of excitement. After sending a flush up my neck with her artful manipulation, she turned me around forcefully, one hand on my shoulder, the other dipping down under my skirt and deftly into my panties. I was almost embarrassed by how wet I was; her finger slid easily and quickly into me.

She bent down, as though patting me down for weapons, lifted my skirt, and buried her face between my legs. I felt weak in the knees, but managed to stay upright, leaning back onto the hood of the Mini and raising one leg to give her better access.

The guy cop wasn't just standing idly by as all this happened. He was stroking his big purple monster and had his hand on the back of his partner's head, urging her to lick and suck on my clit, not that she seemed to need any help.

I don't know how he managed it, but he climbed up on the hood, straddled me, pushed up my shirt, pulled down my bra, and slid that veined pulsating cock of his between my soft cushiony tits. He pushed them together, holding them with one masterful hand, pulling my nipples.

She was still working feverishly on my clit, fingers buried inside me, pressing and pushing until I thought I'd scream or faint, or both. When I came, I nearly drenched her with my juice. She stood up, proudly displaying her wet, shiny face. She then leaned back against the car right next to me, undid her top, and exposed her impressive breasts. They were giant mounds of soft flesh with angry red nipples that seemed hard enough to poke out an eye. Her partner reached over with his free hand and started massaging and pulling at her breasts. She stuck her hand down her pants and started fingering herself, really going to town. Her hair had come loose and was blowing wildly in the wind and I could see her eyes rolling back as she started to come. Once she came, he got down off the car, pulled me to standing, and guided my hand to his gorgeous staff. I eagerly took hold and started jacking him off as he continued to graze her tits with his fingertips.

He started to rock back and forth and through gritted teeth he demanded I drop to my knees. He didn't have to ask twice. I gobbled up his huge cock, deep-throating him with abandon. It took just a few good hard pulls and he threw back his head and let out a roar as he came in me.

He helped me to my feet as his partner was already buttoning up and pulling her hair back into place. She smacked me on the ass as she walked to her bike without saying a word to either of us. He helped me back into my car, gave me my license and registration, and with a "drive carefully, ma'am," tipped an imaginary hat to me and walked back to his bike.

I must have sat there stunned for a good ten minutes after they had both ridden off. Finally, I pulled myself together, checked my face in the mirror to make sure I looked presentable, and started the car. I looked out for any sign of them the whole rest of that ride, and on every ride I've taken through that canyon since, but I've never seen them again. However, every time I see a motorcycle cop, I tend to speed up a little in hopes he'll pull me over and push me down.

Pilar Lopez

Clear Communications

I was in the lobby of the hotel where I work as an engineer. My job is the wiring of the communications systems, which means I am in charge of the Internet, cable, telephone, and so on.

Anyway, this shapely blonde in a bikini and white cover-up that didn't cover a damn thing walked up to me while I was reviewing some charts.

"Is the beer in the bar cold?" she asked.

Though it was an incredibly odd question, I told her "Absolutely. Coldest, wettest thing around."

She smiled and said, "Coldest, sure, but I bet it isn't the wettest."

Then she walked off and I, puzzled by the exchange, tried to go on with my work.

The next day she stopped me in the lobby again. She was definitely hot, if a little strange.

I wear a uniform that clearly identifies me as an engineer and yet she stopped again to ask me questions.

"Where is the spa?"

There was a sign right in front of her pointing the way. I showed it to her and was going to go about my work when she interrupted again.

"Can I get a good massage from a man with really strong hands who knows what he's doing there?"

I was a little surprised by her questions, but I do work for the hotel and they are constantly telling us that we are all "ambassadors" for the company.

"I don't really know the people who work in the spa, but I'm sure you can get what you want," I replied.

"Oh! It's not just that I want it, I really, really need it," she breathed.

She slipped her hand through my arm and leaned against me, asking me to walk her down to the spa so she could see about an appointment. She said she didn't want to get lost.

I know that blondes aren't really dumb, but this one sure was playing dumb. The sign pointed right down the hall and you could almost see the spa from where we stood, but I wasn't about to be rude, especially as she was pressing her round tits into me.

I walked her to the spa. Once there, she said she'd come back to make her appointment later. She asked me then to show her the pool and workout area. This was way outside my job description, but I figured, what the hell. Here was this hot, sexy woman touching me and being suggestive, and I couldn't help but look at her wet mouth and glossy lips and imagine burying my cock in there.

"So, I take it your job isn't to show me around," she said, as we ended our little tour. "And you aren't a professional masseuse, either, are you?"

I explained that I keep systems on track and look into problems with the rooms that might be communications related, like no Internet connection, problems with the television and phone, that sort of thing. She told me she'd been having all sorts of communications problems. I told her to report it to the front desk and they would likely send me to look into it.

I hadn't been back on the job more than a couple minutes when I got a job call to go check on the Internet, television, and phone in the penthouse suite.

I was pretty impressed that this sexy but ditzy woman was staying in the penthouse. On my way up, I wondered what I would find but determined to focus on my job and keep it professional, even though I really just wanted to get her down on her knees and bury my dick in her cherry-red mouth.

I knocked on her door and announced who I was. When she opened the door she was standing there as naked as she could be. So much for professionalism.

As I entered the room, I noticed that there was an adult film playing on the television. Seems it was working just fine. Guess she wasn't really having the sort of problems that I'd need my tool belt for, though I sure hoped I would get to use my tool to fix her up.

"So, miss, just what sort of communication problems are you having?" I asked, trying not to stare at her incredible body.

"I want to be fucked unconscious and I wasn't sure my message was getting through." She purred as she cupped my crotch and licked her lips.

She planted a very wet kiss on my lips. My cock, already pretty hard, started throbbing as it tried to burst through my zipper. She unzipped my pants and fell to her knees, whipping out my dick. She then started to suck it vigorously.

Her mouth felt even better than I had fantasized. I thought I was going to blow my load right away.

I enjoyed her sucking me for some time, but then had to pull her up and take a little break. I led her to the bed. She lay down, slowly opening her legs, and said, "Please fuck me, I need it so bad!"

"Your message is coming through loud and clear now, miss. I'll see what I can do to make sure you are fully satisfied with your stay with us," I said, as I went down on my knees and brought my mouth to her dripping cunt. I caressed her thighs, hips, and ass, dipping my finger into her asshole, as I sucked that pussy raw. She came suddenly, spurting her juices out all over my chin. It tasted sweet. It was the first time I'd been with a woman who came like that.

I continued to press my finger into her ass and she started really begging me to fuck her.

"Fuck me with your big hard cock. I knew you were the right man for this job the moment I saw you." She grabbed at me, pulling me to her.

As I slid my cock into her come-soaked pussy, I took her tits in my mouth, first one, then the other, sucking on her nipples. When she exploded again, I shot my load into her squirming cunt.

A moment later the lady was down by my crotch, sucking my balls. Then she rolled me over on my stomach and without hesitation stuck her tongue up my ass, licking and probing with truly amazing dexterity. When she turned me back I was hard again, and she crouched over me in a 69 position and set her mouth to work, her tongue stroking from my shaft to my ass. I sucked her clit into my mouth and we ate each other to fucking heaven.

Afterward she said, "I am worried that for some reason the lines may get crossed again. I really need to be sure that my messages are received."

"Don't you worry," I said, "you call me anytime and I'll straighten out whatever seems blocked."

But the next day I learned that she had checked out of the hotel. It wasn't too long after that when I was called by a headhunter firm for the top communications technology group in the Valley for an interview. They had heard I was masterful at my job and wanted to arrange for me to come in immediately to meet with the CTO of the company. In my best suit with a freshly updated résumé, I entered a huge top-floor conference room. At first I thought it was empty. Then the chair at the head of the table swiveled around and a pair of slim, tan, nicely muscled legs propped themselves up on the conference table. Looking up from the legs to the tapping manicured fingernails on the arm of the chair I wasn't totally surprised to find the amazing blonde gazing back at me with a smirk on her lovely face.

"Seems we have a need for a communications expert with real talent and a way of dealing with a hot spot that from my experience was incredibly impressive."

"Well, I hope that I'm your man," I said, clearing my throat and feeling the blood rush to my cock.

"Oh, yes. I do think that you are my man." She pressed a button and the windows darkened, shutting out prying eyes as she stood and walked toward me.

Adina Giordano

I cannot agree enough that fantasies about nasty dirty sex in a run-down disgusting fleabag motel are much better lived out in a clean middle-of-the-road sort of hotel with your imagination filling in the gaps.

Going into Business Together

I've been having a wild, wanton, hot fuck-buddy relationship with the boss for going on eleven years now. We didn't always work together. We met through work, but at different offices in different towns. I would drive four hours to have a marathon of crazy sex every other weekend. He was my first 69, my first tit job, and my first anal. In fact, he's been my only for those, too. We ended up living closer for a bit, then farther apart, then closer again. Finally, after ten years, he started his own company and begged me to work with him. Uninterrupted access on a daily basis to mind-blowing sex and the opportunity to work with someone I really liked and make more money were strong sales points, so I left my career to try it out.

We'd had sex at both our offices in the past. Hell, we'd had sex in the company car when going on joint meetings, in the service elevator when he helped me move into a new building, at a holiday party in the bathroom of the CEO's house, and too many other wild places for me to list. What we hadn't ever had was regular, anytime we want it, sex. And it was killing the lust.

Who knew that having the opportunity to have sex every day without fear of interruption or worrying about being found out would so quickly and so thoroughly destroy the insatiability of our desire? Without having to plan and sneak and be illicit, we started arranging time in the calendar, between sales calls, to have a quickie.

It used to be that I'd suck him off, tonguing his balls and teasing him mercilessly as he made that call, or he'd have me bent over, running his long, hard cock in and out of my pussy while he pushed his thumb in my ass while I tried to speak normally to a client. Now that it was his company and we were more or less partners in business, the sex was placed on a back burner. At first it was set at simmer until eventually, it was more like Great-aunt Edna's turkey soup, frozen and buried in the back of the freezer.

Business was good, good and growing. It was growing so fast that he needed to bring in more people. He expanded the space to add a large office where he housed two marketing people to help bring in new business and keep in touch with the current clients. The marketing team was made up of two hot young women pretty much only a year or two out of college. They both had long-term boyfriends and I know you think you know where this story is going, but you're wrong on all counts.

He didn't start fucking one of these leggy, sexy goddesses only to have the other walk in and join them. He didn't fuck them together and have me catch him and then get all hot and horny and start fingering myself to climax. I didn't get into some wet, slippery girl-on-girl thing or seduce one or both of these young lovelies with a couple glasses of cheap chardonnay and then let him have my seconds. Not that I doubt for a second that he harbored fantasies or deny that I may have played around a little with ones of my own.

No, what did happen is that because of the layout and lack of privacy, we had to start sneaking around and finding times and ways to get each other off again. It was perfect.

They'd take off for lunch, and we wouldn't know if they were grabbing a quick burrito from down the street and coming back to eat at the office or going to the sushi place and planning on being gone for at least an hour. But as soon as that front door closed, he'd be rubbing against me, grabbing my tits from behind, grinding his hard cock into my ass through our clothes and whispering disgusting, nasty, tidbits in my ear about what he was going to do to me, turning me on and making me a gushing fountain of wetness, aching for him and clutching at my clit, panting and out of breath.

We tried getting to the office early to meet and have a quickie, only to have one of us get caught in traffic or last-minute home stuff. We tried putting them on a big project and getting each other off in the storage area. We told them we had strategy planning to do and to knock before coming into the office, but the layout was so weird and open, there wasn't really anyplace we could go. The bathroom was between his office and their office and you could hear the soap dispenser squirt the walls were so thin. Plus, they would totally have noticed if we both went in at the same time. While we like sneaking around and the threat of getting caught, we don't really actually want to get caught, so basically, the office became off limits or we had to get down and dirty with a quickie to be sure we'd get things done before one or both girls returned.

We started going for drives for lunch and I'd give him a mind-blowing cock suck and tug as he tried to keep focused on traffic. We'd park down the road at the park overlooking the river and have a serious heavy-petting session. We rented a room at a fleabag motel in the industrial area not too far from our offices where we acted out the cheap crack-whore fantasy, which really is much better to act out in a cleaner place since I'm not actually a crack whore and I was afraid of touching anything, including the faucets to wash my hands after touching the tabletop and doorknob. We even started planning out-of-town business trips, just so we could slip into each other's rooms and have a good six hours or so to pull out the toys, lube, plugs, dongs, costumes, lingerie, etc.

Anyway, I am thrilled to say that working together has turned out to be the fuckfest fantasy we had hoped; it just took hiring more people and sneaking around again to make it interesting.

Bridget O'Leary

JennaTip #5: Hard at Work

Just like in this story, what tends to make work affairs so damn sexy is the fact that they are frowned upon, illicit, forbidden even, and require sneaking around and lying. The sneaking and lying requires a certain amount of creativity and actually accomplishing the act takes planning.

As with elevators, you have to think things through. In the course of thinking it through, you hopefully get caught up in fantasizing about the actual event, fantasizing about shoving up a skirt or undoing a tie, tearing stockings, and throwing away ruined panties.

Favorite locations are a storage room, the bathroom (look for a *family* bathroom if there is one), under, behind, or on top of a desk (not a cubicle, please), in the stairwell, in the car lot, while she bends over to file papers in the lower cabinet, in the copier room, and after hours on top of the desk of the guy who really ticks you off, leaving your used sex rag or tissues in his wastebasket hoping the stink of sex permeates his office and drives him nuts.

Places not to have office sex include on the break table because everyone eats off it, including you (although that might be a turn-on for you, after all), in front of a security camera, in a common room like a conference room that anyone might pop into and which generally is centrally located in the office with lots of pedestrian traffic.

Finally, you should arrange business lunches that allow you time away from the office, business trips, particularly the overnight type, and the crème de la crème is at the office party at the boss's house, having sex in the guest bathroom and using the good hand towels to clean up after, leaving your torn stockings and sopping panties balled up in the sink because he's a cheap bastard who stiffed you on your year-end bonus.

If every girl had a friend like this the world would be such a better, sexier place.

Educating Zoe

Zoe and Jack have an average sex life. They will celebrate their eleventh wedding anniversary months before the end of this story. They will enjoy weekly, hour-long lovemaking sessions in the missionary position with the closet light on but the covers pulled up for at least fifty-two more weeks before we're done with this tale.

Zoe is very attractive and a lot of fun. She's also always been a bit of a prude. Jack at one point was a little on the wild side but eleven years with the same woman and he has forgotten most of the little he ever knew. Wild for him, since he was still quite young, meant having a woman on top or trying it doggie style. Zoe and Jack married so young, he didn't know how to ask for what he wanted and because of her being quite reserved, he hadn't learned or tried to learn. He'd never even had the chance for some good 69 action before he and Zoe were dating, then in love, then married. Over the years, he'd watched some clandestine porn now and again and with the burgeoning world of Internet porn, he'd surfed enough to know that an entire world existed outside his pleasant bedroom. He'd tried to introduce some new experiences, but with very little luck. He was all but resigned to nice married sex in a mostly dark bedroom interspersed with jack-off sessions as he fantasized about his pretty Zoe getting down on her knees and licking his balls, letting him come all over her face and breasts.

Zoe for her part knew something was missing; she just didn't know how to add it. She thought of herself as a good cook but not a chef. A cook follows the recipe and everything comes out as it should. A chef sprinkles a little here, adds some there until what you've got is a bubbling hot, mouth-watering religious experience for your senses. Zoe desperately wanted to be a chef in their love life, not the good cook she was. Being determined and from strong New England stock, Zoe set about to make the change.

Zoe bought books. Well, she didn't buy at first. At first she went to the store at its least busy time and went to the sexuality section, grabbed a couple of books off the shelves, then hid away in a corner browsing and looking, hoping for inspiration. Finally, she broke down and bought a few books and read them while on the toilet, hoping Jack wouldn't think she had some weird stomach problems because she would be locked away in the bathroom for thirty to forty minutes at a time. If she could fig-ure a way to dye her hair at the same time or wax her legs, then she knew she'd have a good excuse, but she just wasn't up to the challenge of figuring out the positions described in the book and applying hot wax and linen to her thigh at the same time.

When the books didn't seem to be helping very much, Zoe tried watching porn. She searched porn on her computer, terri-fied the entire time that she'd be caught and then overwhelmed and horrified when she couldn't get the sites to close after they kept opening one after another, most with sounds of people moaning and screaming. Damn, but she should have turned the sound off, but at least Jack was out mowing the lawn. At least she prayed he was still out mowing the lawn. She wanted to get up to look, but what if he wasn't and he came in while the sounds and pop-ups were still tormenting her? She unplugged her computer, vowing not to search porn ever again. What she had seen had been so far out of her league it was like taking someone who could make chocolate cookies by breaking apart the precut squares and putting them on a cookie sheet and placing them in the oven for twelve minutes and expecting them to make a flaming bananas Foster while blindfolded and dancing the Macarena.

Zoe continued on at a complete loss. Then one evening at her book group the women she's known and talked to at least on a monthly if not more often basis start talking about the sex in one of their recent books. Normally the sex is pretty generic or behind closed doors, but this book had been selected by a new member and the sex had been really quite hot and right out in the open. It is an awakening for the club and Zoe learns that these women are truly a font of knowledge, untapped heretofore.

She tries not to betray her ignorance, but time and again someone asks her what she thinks in the midst of their heated and hot conversation and she blushes and mumbles and often says something so off topic that very soon it becomes clear to one and all, that except for missionary-position sex, Zoe is a virgin.

Instead of laughing or teasing, as Zoe expects, these women pet her and act like she's just lost her favorite cat. Then the questions start.

Does she orgasm?

Does she never give head?

What about a hand job?

Does she masturbate?

Doesn't he go down on her?

Zoe stutters her answers, mostly just shaking her head no, no, and no again. The women are all ready to lynch Jack when Zoe finally finds her voice and explains that Jack wants her to orgasm and he wants to go down on her, that he bought her a massaging showerhead and tried to give her a bath and is very attentive. She said it isn't him, not him at all, but her. She just doesn't know how to do any of it and is afraid to do it wrong and so she just shuts off that side of her desire and does her best to make box macaroni and cheese rather than cheese soufflé.

Oh, darling, you can't do it wrong.

It absolutely isn't like cooking at all, silly.

If crack heads can do it well enough to make money at it, of course you can, too.

The last comment was from the new member, Alyssa, the one who'd recommended the book in the first place. She is the youngest in the group and from the city and a new transplant and not a mother and kept her own name when she married.

It is Alyssa who takes charge of Zoe and her education at that moment. The other women, rather than feeling she is overstepping, encourage her, as she is, as they all believe, the most likely suspect when it comes to being the sex expert in the crowd, though Madge, in her fifties, isn't any shrinking violet—they all know that from certain stories she shares when having a second glass of wine. But Madge isn't the right one for helping Zoe; of this everyone is sure. Zoe is just about thirty-three and her one little boy is turning five while Madge is fifty-seven if a day and a grandmother seven times over and also on her second husband, her first having died of a massive heart attack on their twenty-third wedding anniversary while in the throes of passion. As noted before, Madge is no shrinking violet.

And so the education of Zoe begins. Alyssa and Zoe start having lunch at Alyssa's place once a week. Alyssa starts with books and pictures, moves up to film, then shows Zoe how to search on the Internet and find useful and informative pages about sex rather than porn video loops of big cocks in barely legal girls' mouths, which is what Zoe had found in her one disastrous search.

Alyssa helps Zoe peel a cucumber, then suck on it until she fits it deep into her mouth without throwing up. Alyssa explains to Zoe about the prostate, about the taint, about gently handling and kissing and also sucking on a guy's balls. She talks to Zoe about the anus. She talks about putting in a finger or just pressing on the pucker. She talks about rimming and licking and sticking in the tongue, too. She tells Zoe about doggie style, being on top, being the reverse cowgirl, 69, and even spooning, shocked that Zoe hasn't at least tried spooning, but not making her feel like a freak about it.

Alyssa explains about the clitoris, the G-spot, nipples, and toes. She buys Zoe a little pocket vibrator and encourages her to try it out. When Zoe just cannot use the vibrator, she convinces Zoe to get herself drunk and try again. It works a little better the second time except Zoe is too drunk and falls asleep. Zoe is so thankful that Jack is gone on a fishing trip with their little boy when this happens. She can just imagine Jack finding her passed out from too much wine with a still going vibrator clutched in her hand and her nightie hiked up to her stomach.

Finally, Zoe squeaks out a little orgasm in the tub with her massaging shower head after just one glass of wine and lots of coaching and encouragement from Alyssa.

Zoe makes great strides, yet there is no change in her relations with Jack. He's given up, just as she decides it is time to take the bull by the horns. She doesn't have the slightest idea how to let him know she is changing, she is willing, and she is ready.

Alyssa asks one day how things are going and is floored by the salty big tears that burst from Zoe's eyes. Through sobs and hiccups, Zoe finally admits she just doesn't know how to bring it up and is terrified to touch him differently and suck on his penis or anything because she just knows she'll do it wrong.

So the plan is all Alyssa's. It is daring. It is dangerous. It is daunting. Zoe is sure she will never be able to go through with it, but she also knows, deep down she does know, that if she doesn't try that eventually, she and Jack will drift apart, they'll have less and less sex, they'll each harbor resentments because neither is trying or talking anymore, and then it will be a lonely, dusty, dry, dismal marriage or a sad, pathetic, unnecessary divorce. Zoe just does not want her life to be like that.

Jack owns a boat. He likes to fish. He likes to just go cruising for the afternoon. Zoe often goes along, relaxing in the sunshine. Though she is something of a prude, Zoe does have a lovely figure and shows it off for Jack, wearing skimpy bathing suits and occasionally removing her top, though not often enough for Jack. Jack learned long ago that if Zoe is aware he is watching her, looking longingly at her, and desiring her, she will put her top back on, sit up, and start talking about catching fish, cleaning them, gutting them, and whatever else she can think of that will turn his mind away from her body and away from their bodies together.

As it is the end of the season, it is do-or-die time for the plan. Zoe invites her new and closest friend Alyssa to join her on a day trip with Jack on the boat. Jack thinks nothing of it. It is the first time Zoe has done something like this, but she's actually been doing a lot of things recently that are firsts for her. Jack has noticed some of them, but not said anything because he hasn't really been paying all that much attention.

Jack and Zoe meet Alyssa at the harbor in the morning. Zoe has on a skimpy bikini under a pair of shorts and a tank top. Alyssa is similarly dressed. Jack looks at Alyssa appreciatively, hoping Zoe won't see him. Zoe not only sees him looking at Alyssa, she welcomes it. It helps her to think that she is not the center of his attention. That someone else is sharing her burden.

Alyssa realized this quickly in their sessions. Zoe hates being the center. She prefers to be peripheral. Alyssa's plan is to help Zoe bring herself into focus, learn at the same time how to focus as well and not shrink away from sex, from the body, from love.

Once Jack steers them clear of the harbor, Zoe opens a bottle of wine and pours generous glasses for herself and for Alyssa. Jack again notices that this is a first for Zoe, but again Jack isn't paying enough attention to realize that all these firsts are adding up to something big.

When Zoe opens a second bottle because she and Alyssa finish the first, Jack starts to pay a little more attention. Zoe is not a big drinker. She is barely a small drinker. For her to drink on the boat is extremely rare. For her to have more than two glasses at any time is extraordinary.

Zoe is relaxed by the wine, which is very important as she is nervous and wound up because she has made a plan with Alyssa, a plan that requires her to be loose and focused at once. She is terrified to implement the plan. Desperation has driven her to it, because though she is making tremendous strides in her education, she is like a lonely graduate student stuck in a cubby in the library theorizing instead of experiencing. She is like a cook who reads recipes in gourmet magazines but never buys the ingredients or tries to make any of the dishes.

Zoe suggests an obscure cove as a lovely place to anchor for a swim and lunch. Jack agrees and soon they are all sitting on the deck enjoying the gentle sway of the boat, considering jumping in to cool off but being too warm and lazy to do so. Zoe and Alyssa remove their shorts, they remove their tank tops, and it seems to Jack that all at once they also remove their bathing-suit tops. He shakes his head once, twice, a third time like a dog with water in its ears, then rubs the heels of his hands into his eyes, attempting to clear them and see reality because seeing Zoe topless with her friend Alyssa also topless, sitting on his boat, in the middle of the day must be a hallucination.

It isn't a hallucination. Zoe and Alyssa have their tops off. They are sitting up kicking at the water and chatting happily to one another and they have no tops on to conceal their breasts. Zoe would not sit up. She would not kick the water. Zoe would be self-conscious and at the slightest hint that Jack was looking at her, cover up. But this Zoe, this Zoe sitting next to Alyssa, is aware Jack has noticed them but the imperative word is *them* because it means that Jack does see her, but he also sees Alyssa. Zoe is not alone.

Zoe dips her finger into her glass of wine, lifts her finger to her lips, inserts it between them and sucks the moisture off. Jack stays incredibly still as though having just spotted a rare and incredibly skittish and beautiful bird perched inches from him and afraid to breathe for fear it will startle and vanish before he can study the intricacies of its plumage.

Zoe and Alyssa, however, are at ease and clearly enjoying the warm sun caressing their skin, the light breeze kissing their nipples, the play of sunlight on the dancing water. Alyssa caresses Zoe's neck and back, then leans against her with her arm draped across her shoulders like best friends, thinks Jack, or lovers, he thinks again. His cock stirs, thinking farther along those lines than Jack is conscious of, at least for a moment, before his brain catches up and sees the same image his cock already has conjured of the women embracing in a passionate kiss that turns into one or the other working her way down to between her friend's legs, though Jack is confused as to which woman he wants to see most in which position until her realizes he can switch back and forth in his imagination and enjoy his fantasy both ways.

In reality, the women are simply sitting and talking softly to one another. Zoe feels her friend touch her. It relaxes her. She feels sexy and attractive and loved. Since Jack is staring at her but Alyssa is touching her, she is distracted from feeling over-whelmed by the attention.

Jack, lost in his lusty daydream, doesn't bother to think that there is a deeper meaning to this, that it is anything other than a slight bump in his calm, prosaic life. If he took a step back, he would think that perhaps there was a conspiracy between Zoe and Alyssa, one that involved him. But he didn't think deeply on this or most occasions lately. Jack was so busy thinking that life was settled and Zoe was Zoe that he was missing the changes in her. She knew she was changing. She just didn't know how to wake Jack up to enjoy those changes. If her plan with Alyssa failed to break through she was at her wits' end as to how to jump-start their marriage and get it out of the rut it was in and onto the racetrack she craved.

Zoe and Alyssa stop talking. It takes Jack a moment to realize what is different as he is still lost in his precoital haze of fantasy. The women look frankly at him, at his tented shorts. Alyssa nudges Zoe. Zoe frowns at Alyssa. Alyssa nods her head with en-couragement as she looks meaningfully at Zoe and then at Jack and then back to Zoe. Zoe stands. She walks to Jack. She kneels down in front of him. Zoe looks over her shoulder at her friend. She turns back to Jack, who watches mesmerized as she puts her fingers into the waistband of his shorts. She pulls down, down, down until he adjusts and allows them to slide over his hips and ass. He is exposed, his cock bobbing and weaving drunkenly in front of Zoe. Her eyes never leave it, not until she finds herself going cross-eyed as her mouth wraps around the head of it, then she looks up-ward, up to Jack's shocked face. He is now paying full and close attention to Zoe. She freezes. Alyssa comes behind her. Alyssa puts her arms around her. Alyssa whispers in her ear and runs her hands down her back. Zoe takes a deep breath. She continues.

Zoe licks Jack's cock from the base right near his balls to just under the head, to the scar from his circumcision. She drags her tongue flattened over the head once, then, squeezing her lips firmly around his cock, lowers her head to engulf the entire rigid length in her wet and warm mouth. Once her lips are at the base of Jack's happily surprised penis, Zoe opens her mouth and exhales before pulling her head back up, barely grazing Jack as she does. She sits back on her heels, turns to her left, and glances over her shoulder at Alyssa, then asks, "Does it always twitch like that?"

Alyssa nods, saying, "In my vast experience, yes, it will always twitch and wiggle about unless you grasp it firmly in your hand."

Jack is speechless.

"Remember, Zoe, you have to love his cock. Don't think of Jack, think of his cock. The cock loves you and you love the cock. You are kissing the cock to show how much you adore it. Whisper to it. Now."

Zoe turns back to Jack's cock. She grasps it gently in her hand. She leans in, places her lips at the very tip, and whispers softly to it. As she keeps whispering, she strokes the cock, petting it, and then she kisses it lovingly. She kisses it under its head, along its shaft, and back up on the very tip of it. She puts her tongue out and tastes the edge of it, licking it as though French kissing it, as though the penis kisses her back, whispers back, loves her back. It does.

"Excellent work, Zoe. I am so proud of you." Alyssa stands and comes closer, looking down at Zoe cradling the cock in her hands, stroking it and sucking on it happily. "Aren't you proud of her, Jack?"

"Huh." Jack is still not quite in the moment.

"Jack. Your beautiful, sexy, amazing, loving, adoring, incredible wife has spent months educating herself and learning to let go of her fears to better love you, to find a way for you to better love her, for her to accept your love physically." Alyssa stood, topless, hands on hips almost lecturing Jack but with a smile softening her tone and words. "She's amazing, isn't she, Jack?"

"She's the most amazing, this is the most amazing . . ." Jack tries to express himself, but Zoe continues to caress his cock and has suckled his left testicle into her warm mouth and is running her tongue over its contours and he is distracted again.

Alyssa moves to stand behind Jack. She looks down at Zoe, watches her head bobbing up and down. Alyssa leans down and whispers in Jack's ear. She whispers to him the details of Zoe's education. Of the books and videos and vegetables that Zoe has spent months poring over and practicing with in order to finally, today, invite Jack to join her on this journey. Jack is drunk, not on wine, but on the feelings he is experiencing. His head lolls back against Alyssa's plump and naked breasts. He reaches for her, but she steps away. While she and Zoe agreed that Alyssa should be there, should make herself available as a coach, a mentor, a surrogate if Zoe could not go through with the plan, Zoe is mastering the plan and Alyssa, with all confidence in her pet project, carefully pulls her tank top back on and takes herself belowdecks, leaving Zoe to pass her final exam alone with her husband, Jack.

Zoe pinches the loose skin of the ball sack between her finger and thumb. She pulls down and she licks up. She grasps the base of his cock and mumbles around the head. She lets her spit flow freely down and over his cock until it nestles, glistening in the hairs where his cock meets his body. Jack's breath comes in great ragged gasps. Zoe waits a moment. She stands. She steps forward so that she straddles Jack. She lowers herself to his waiting lap. She impales herself upon his cock, pulls Jack in to have his head and lips pressed to her breasts. She twists and thrusts. He opens his mouth and she buries her nipple inside it. She lifts and lowers herself, up and down on his lap and his cock. She does this again. Zoe pauses. She stands and turns around. She lowers herself with her back to Jack. She sits up leaning against him, lifts his hands, encourages him to caress and touch her breasts. She puts her hand down to her clitoris. She touches him where he enters her. She touches herself. She leans far forward until she puts her hands down to the deck. She moves her hips first one way, then another. She sits back up and plays with her clitoris some more. She grabs Jack's hand and helps him put his finger on her clitoris. She cries out. She arches her back. She throws back her head and rests it against his, rests it on his shoulder. She shudders and twitches. Zoe comes.

When her breath returns to her, Zoe turns around to face Jack, who has sat still, unmoving, amazed and emotional. Jack has not come. Zoe invites Jack to stand, to sit, to recline on the deck with her and to enter her as she sits above him. She rotates her hips and puts her hands on either side of his face and her breasts dance and move with her body. She climbs back off. She turns around. She invites him to penetrate her from behind, to thrust into her as he grasps her hips, to feel the cushion of her firm ass bounce against him as he pushes harder and faster into her, trying for all his being to climb up into her through his penis.

As Jack is about to come, Zoe pulls herself away. Zoe turns around and puts her lips and mouth at his penis. Jack comes. Jack comes on her lips, on her tongue, on her neck and chest. Zoe smiles and laughs and licks him and swallows and rubs his come around on her skin. She kneels up to face him. They both kneel on the deck. She wraps her arms around Jack and kisses him, pressing against him, into him. She laughs again. Jack smiles, then laughs, then hugs and kisses her back.

Zoe and Jack find their way together from this point on, inventing things to do that in the end, should Zoe tell Alyssa, would shock even the unflappable woman who would find her student now a master, no longer a simple cook, but a chef.

Christiana Dalke

JennaTip #6: Getting Good Guidance

If the spark that once lit your fire now barely lights a candle, perhaps it's time to get some professional assistance. The American Association of Sex Educators, Counselors, and Therapists (aasect.org) is a great place to start if you are looking for an expert to rekindle the blaze.

Not yet ready for your own personal sex coach to help you figure out how to make a bonfire? Try the following tips for amazing results.

Foreplay: Just because you've been together forever doesn't mean you can skip the niceties of a little foreplay or a lot of foreplay. Don't just go for the wham and bam act when you can rediscover or discover for the first time a whole slew of erogenous zones such as the earlobe, the back of the thighs, between the toes, the wrist, the scalp . . . really, if it feels good to you and makes you relax and perhaps a bit horny, then that's an erogenous zone for you, even if it isn't for anyone else.

Sex: Redefine it. Sex doesn't have to be intercourse. Sex doesn't have to be an orgasm (his or hers). Sex can be an extension of foreplay. Sex can be phone sex. It can be putting naked pictures of yourself in your partner's lunch with a note explaining exactly what you want to do later or exactly what you were doing when the photo was taken or exactly what you are doing right now at lunchtime thinking of your partner finding and looking at the photo. Sex can be massage, a bath, an ice rubdown, undressing or dressing up. Don't limit your sex life, but be open to the possibilities.

Make an Effort: Unless your partner wants it dirty and nasty, take a shower, use deodorant, shave, brush your teeth, brush your tongue, and brush your hair. Bathe one another. Brush her hair, shave his jaw, and massage scented oils into each other. You may notice that this seems a lot like foreplay. I wonder why that is?

Take Turns: If your partner normally is the one to initiate sex, borrow that role and be the aggressor. If you do all the heavy lifting when it comes to foreplay, pass the torch, lie back, put your feet up, and give your lover a chance to show off.

Talk: Talk about what you want. Talk about what you need. Talk about who you want to pretend to be. Talk about the hot neighbor you'd like to soap up next time there's a neighborhood car wash. Talk about sex. Do not talk about bills, dentist appointments (unless that's a turn-on for you), or whose turn it is to change the cat litter. Talk about talking more.

Score! Stop keeping score. This is not a game. There is no competition. You are on the same team. There is no goal except pleasure. Orgasm is not the end all and be all. It is the journey to orgasm, the trek you take together, and the joy you take in bringing each other to orgasm that matters. If all you need is an orgasm, then do it yourself, after all.

Feeling Neighborly

After eighteen years of marriage it was finally time for Beth to fulfill a fantasy both she and Gary had savored over those years. Beth was finally going to know what it was like to touch, kiss, lick, and love a woman. And Gary was going to get to watch. Watch and join in, of course.

The thought of seeing his sweet, pretty Beth with her face buried between a woman's quivering thighs, tongue lapping her sopping bush, caused his gut to roll over with anticipation as his cock bobbed in his pants. He had to excuse himself from several morning sales meetings over the weeks as they planned the event to take care of himself in the bathroom or risk exploding and making a mess.

Gary would pull his monstrous, hard cock out and stroke it while imagining burying it in his wife's sweet pussy from behind as her face was buried between another woman's legs. He imagined watching this other woman's face as she came, grabbing her own breasts and squeezing them hard, head thrown back. It only took a few good, hard, long pulls before he'd come. He'd return to the meeting, face flushed, as though he had climbed the fourteen flights of stairs to his office, and attempt to keep his mind on projections and numbers for at least another day.

Beth knew it would be a little tricky arranging this tryst, what with the two kids and the small, close-knit neighborhood, but perhaps the close-knit neighborhood would prove a positive factor rather than an obstacle. The kids had plenty of friends they could spend the night or weekend with, leaving Beth and Gary free to engage in hours of uninterrupted pleasure.

In addition, there was a new, single woman neighbor with the hottest body just next door who had been really friendly the times they'd seen her at neighborhood gatherings. She also just happened to leave her blinds open while exercising in her upstairs workout room, immediately across from their bedroom, and she exercised nude.

Beth was entranced by her fabulous curves and fantasized about licking and sucking her pink nipples while the woman caressed her hips and ass in a loving embrace. Beth imagined that while Gary was very male with his hairy chest, rough beard, musky odor, and callused hands, being with a woman would be all soft skin and sweet scents.

"Women must be pure pleasure to kiss," Beth thought, with their plump, soft lips and gentle tongues.

Their neighbor tended to relax after a hot, sweaty workout with a series of mind-blowing orgasms, based on what Beth and Gary could see while peeping through their blinds. Gary often asked Beth to describe what was happening as he was usually too busy licking and sucking Beth's wet cunt.

Beth told Gary that the "tramp from next door," as they liked to call her because it made them both feel naughty and dirty, turning them on, would stand in front of the mirrors caressing her swollen breasts, lifting a rosy nipple up to her mouth and biting and tonguing herself. Beth told him how she pushed her fingers into her pussy, licking them clean, savoring each drip. She told him how even though her head was a mane of raven tresses, her pussy lips had only a tiny little strip of hair. "Like a landing strip for your tongue," Beth liked to say.

The neighbor had a thin, long dildo that she inserted expertly into her ass, watching her reflection in the mirror the entire time, giving Beth plenty of ideas that she and Gary could act out together. Her name was Veronica.

Beth arranged for the kids to spend from Saturday morning until Sunday evening at a friend's house and then invited Veronica for drinks for Saturday afternoon, suggesting she stay over for dinner and make an evening of it. Beth and Gary wanted all day Saturday to prepare. They also were so damn horny they wanted to fuck themselves unconscious and have time to recover to do it all over again, only this time with Veronica.

Veronica arrived right on time, holding a pitcher of margaritas and three big glasses. She was in a short button-front little dress that clung to her curves, showing off her fantastic shape. She handed the drinks to Gary, gave Beth a big hug and squeeze, then said she had to run back to her place to get the salt for the glasses and some spicy salsa she'd whipped up.

Beth, who was also in a little summery dress with a low-cut front and flirty skirt, stuck a finger into the pitcher, pulled it out, and licked it clean. "Wow," Beth warned Gary, "Veronica must have used twice the usual tequila in these. We'll have to be careful to get loose without losing it."

Veronica popped back over, salted the glasses, filled them to the rim, and offered a toast to her hosts.

"To neighbors getting closer."

"We'll drink to that," Beth said, tilting his drink for a sip and giving Gary a secret smile.

"To hot salsa, hot nights, and hot times with hot women." Gary joked. Veronica laughed, took a big drink, and as she passed by Gary to get her chips and salsa, ran a red-tipped fingernail along his chest, smiling and licking her lips as she said:

"I assure you, Beth and I are both a lot hotter than this salsa, and I used fresh jalapeños."

Beth and Veronica got settled on the love seat while Gary stood at the bar between the kitchen and living room, just looking at them as he sipped his drink. Both women's dresses showed tons of leg. Beth ran a hand up Veronica's bare leg to her thigh.

"You have the smoothest legs. How do you get them so soft?" Beth asked.

"It's a special shea butter bar I use. It smells divine, too." Veronica purred as she placed her hand on top of Beth's, holding it to her thigh.

"Mind if I check?" Beth leaned over to sniff at Veronica's thigh. "Mmmm. Smells like dessert." Then, before she lost her nerve, Beth licked Veronica's leg. "Mmmm. Tastes like dessert, too."

Veronica shivered and twitched at the feel of Beth's gentle caress. She licked her lips, saying, "I never tasted it before myself. I'll have to try that sometime."

"Hey, what about me? I'm starving over here." Gary joked. He walked over and settled in on the love seat on Veronica's other side, squeezing them all together, ran his hand up her thigh, leaned down for a good sniff and also licked her leg, all the way from her knee up to the hem of her dress, pushing it up a bit with his nose to lick farther.

Veronica moaned as she became drenched from this unexpected and extremely arousing experience.

"I take it that the invite wasn't just for dinner?" Veronica managed to gasp out as Beth's hand traveled up under her dress and her fingers lightly brushed Veronica's mound through her panties.

"Well, we thought maybe you'd be dessert. Since we haven't eaten yet, you'll just have to be dinner as well, 'cause I'm starving."

That being said, Beth dropped from the seat to her knees, pushed up Veronica's skirt, and nosed aside the filmy panties to give her full access to Veronica's hot, wet pussy. Beth was amazed at how sweet Veronica smelled and tasted. She'd only licked her juices off Gary's fingers, tongue, and chin before and had no idea that a woman would taste so absolutely yummy.

"God. You taste divine." She stopped momentarily to tell Veronica. Veronica, for her part, had her head thrown back and was running her fingers through Beth's hair, eyes closed, her mouth hanging partially open. Gary had stepped back for a better view and had his cock out of his zipper, ready for action at the slightest sign from Beth.

Gary pushed the coffee table out of the way, making a large play area in the center of the room, on the soft, plush rug. He invited the women to make themselves more comfortable and Veronica and Beth moved from the couch to the floor.

"I have to touch your breasts. I've been fantasizing about them for months. You have the greatest nipples," Beth told Veronica.

"How do you know?" Veronica asked, puzzled.

"You don't shut your blinds when you exercise, or after, when you go through your cooldown routine," Beth replied.

Veronica blushed, then slowly unbuttoned her dress, letting it slide from her body, leaving her in her panties and matching bra. Beth pushed the left cup down, exposing Veronica's breast, and fell upon the nipple like a starving woman.

Veronica moaned and started fingering herself. Beth stopped just long enough to look over her shoulder at Gary and invite him to lick her own pussy juices as she knew that she was close but wanted to focus her tongue and fingers on Veronica. As Veronica slipped two and then three fingers inside herself and thumbed her clit, Gary sucked and licked Beth's twat from her ass to her clit, burying his face between her legs. Beth fondled Veronica's other breast, licked and bit her nipple, and with her other hand reached around, driving her finger up into Veronica's ass, pushing her over the brink and making her scream with a soul-shattering orgasm.

"I'm going to come, Gary, and I want to come with your huge cock in me." Beth moaned as she kept fingering Veronica, making her come again and again. Gary, always willing to please, pushed Beth's dress up over her hips, pushed the little slip of a thong out of his way, then savagely rammed his purple-headed cock into her soaking cunt. Veronica used her fingers on herself and then her other hand on Beth, flicking and pulling her clit as Gary expertly fucked his wife until she creamed and almost passed out. He pulled out just as he was about to come and shot his load all over her sweet round ass, then rubbed it around with his cockhead before quickly slipping his still-hard penis into her tight ass. She came again, hard, and collapsed on top of Veronica.

After a few minutes, the three pulled themselves together enough to speak, and Beth, Veronica, and Gary agreed that after a quick meal to get their energy back up, they would go upstairs to the bedroom for the second course in what they all hoped turned into a six- or seven-course meal.

In terms of fulfilling a fantasy, Beth was aching and exhausted by the end of the day Sunday, and never in her wildest dreams would she have been able to imagine the intense pleasure of being with Veronica and Gary together, but she was ready to do it all over again and, in fact, already had arranged for the kids to go away for a full week to see her mother before school started back up. She didn't know how she could wait until then, but Veronica kindly put on a little extra show after her workouts to help her along, smiling across at them as Gary and Beth fucked themselves raw, watching her come.

Adina Giordano

JennaTip #7: The Eyes Have It

voy•eur /*voy-úr, vwä-yúr*/ (*plural* voy•eurs) *n* **1:** Someone who watches for sexual pleasure and gratification; someone who gains pleasure from watching, especially secretly, other people in the nude, dressing or undressing, and/or while engaged in sexual acts.

Doesn't sound very sexy, does it? Read the articles that call it a psychosexual disorder, a paraphilia. Or don't. Instead, think about the time you were staying at a youth hostel in Germany and all the girls were peeking out the second-floor window every morning at 9 A.M. to see the hot guy get off his motor-cycle, circle around to the back of the building behind the bushes, but just below the window, to strip off his clothes and put on his wetsuit to go windsurfing. Remember how you all giggled and pointed and talked and then remember how at night you masturbated by humping your pillow and thinking about this random guy with the incredible washboard stomach and just slightly too long dark hair. That's being a voyeur.

A voyeur is a Peeping Tom who sneaks around backyards trying to look through the half-closed shades, hoping to catch someone, anyone, in the act of taking off clothes. A voyeur is the friend of a friend who waits in the hall for the exact moment you go into the bathroom and then tries to peek under the door or through the lock. The frat boys who ordered pizza and sat on the roof outside the front bedroom and watched as Bob, not his real name, had anal sex with his girlfriend, Kristi, probably her real name, were all voyeurs.

Maybe it is a disorder, but it seems pretty damn widespread with just about all people having some tendency to want to watch, secretly, the object of their lust, at least for that moment in time. As long as you have a relatively *normal* sex life and are able to sustain real world relationships (whatever that means in today's cyber world), then I wouldn't be overly concerned if you find yourself noticing if the guy down the street doesn't always pull his shades before taking a hot shower and sometimes driving a block out of your way to check.

Stripping and peep shows appeal to the voyeur, but they don't include the secretive watching aspect, as the stripper is well aware of the audience. Phone-sex companies often provide recordings of other people having phone sex. The people who listen are considered voyeurs. The people who have been recorded are also aware that people may be listening to them on a recording because they have to agree to a release, otherwise they could sue for invasion of privacy, among other things.

Sure, it isn't very nice to sneak around trying to watch unsuspecting people having sex or changing clothes. It invades their privacy. But since the voyeur does it in secret, the person should never realize their privacy was invaded. If a tree falls in the woods and no one is there to hear it, does it make a noise?

Remember, the only photo that should be taken is a mental one.

Forget about him and just put one of those big vibrating machines between your legs and ride it all night long, particularly in leather chaps.

Boy Toy

Luke woke me with his strong arm reaching over me and his hand gently cupping my breast. His thumb rubbed the tip of my nipple.

I told him, "If this is about some early-morning loving, yes. If you're trying to get round me so I'll agree to you getting a motorbike, my answer is still 'no.'"

To soften my refusal, I reached back and wrapped my fingers around his warm cock.

Luke whispered, "Try it! You'll like it."

"I've heard that line before."

"And you always have—liked it—right?"

"This is different. You know I'm open to new things. I just don't know what we want a bike for. We have a car."

"Just for fun?"

I arched and rubbed the head of his cock against my lips. "*This* is my idea of 'fun.' If you want a boy-toy, how about me?"

I thought I'd distracted him, because he gave a little push, just enough to work the head inside. Then he stopped. I pressed back, but he retreated. Not enough to withdraw, but enough that he went no deeper.

"Tease!" I complained.

His fingers rolled my nipple some more. His teeth closed gently on the nape of my neck, another move that gets my engines revving. Between them, he gritted, "You've never been on a bike.

Come for a test drive. Take one ride with me. If you don't like it, I'll never mention it again. Promise."

"One ride?" I wriggled my hips in his lap.

"Just one."

"Deal! Now can we . . ." I humped back—on nothing! He was scrambling out of bed.

"Where are you going?" I asked, hoping it was to get some bed toys.

"To get a bike."

"But . . . ?" I rolled onto my back and threw the bedclothes aside. Pointing between my legs, I asked, "What about this?"

"*After* the test drive, your sweet little spot will get my undivided attention for as long as you can stand it." And he was gone.

I was miffed. How could Luke *stand* to have his cock's head in me and then stop? He shouldn't have that much control. I thought about taking care of myself right then so that later I could play hard to get. Then I decided on a better plan. I'd stay horny, but I'd make him even hornier. When we got back from riding his silly bike, I'd make him spend three solid hours between my thighs and then I would give him a quick jerk. One ride a day for Luke would just have to be enough.

I dressed in a short thin summer dress that buttoned down the front. Beneath it, there was just me, no bra, and no panties. Against the light, it was translucent. My nipples were perky from me pinching them. I can be *ruthless*!

I stepped out into bright cool sunshine. Luke's handsome head turned toward me. He was sheathed in tight black leather, which really made him look hot. I swayed over to the enormous black-and-chrome machine that sat in our driveway.

He grinned. "You're looking very sexy. Ready for a ride?"

I posed against the sun before I swung a long slender leg over the bike, making sure to give him a flash of my naked bottom. My bare self snuggled down on padded leather. I wriggled around a bit to get myself well placed.

Luke handed me a helmet and kick-started the bike. I almost dropped the helmet, I was so shocked by the powerful vibrations shooting up me.

My arms wrapped around his lean hips. We accelerated away. Our street is paved with cobblestones. Each one was a tiny jolt that felt like hard little slaps, faster and faster until they blended with the throbbing of the engine. My insides became quivering jelly.

I snuggled against him and sucked in the scent of hot leather. My eyes closed. Despite myself, I surrendered to the thrill. It was like I was astride a giant vibrator, set on "high." Wind whipped me. Although I was tight against Luke's back, cold air insinuated its way inside my flimsy dress and nipped my nipples into aching points.

I couldn't help myself. My hips moved. I tilted my ass back a bit and pressed down harder, grinding on a leather seam.

We swung through traffic, leaned past trucks, and were in open country. Now that we wouldn't be observed, I was free to make it even worse for him. My hands pressed his hard thighs and slid upward. My fingers found the zipper of his fly and drew it down. He jerked in surprise but recovered and rocked against my hand! The slut!

My flattened hand slid into his pants. My thumb stroked his muscular belly, hooked his waistband, and dragged his briefs lower. I was rewarded by a fistful of cock, which I carefully drew out. I took a firm but tender grip between my thumb and fingers and began to slow-stroke it in a way I knew would make him desperate but not let him get off.

We sped between fields of wheat.

We must have been doing over one hundred miles an hour when he suddenly decelerated, braked, and swerved. The bike came to a stop. He'd swung off the road into a grove of oaks.

He dismounted. Did he think I was going to put out, then and there? I like the occasional spontaneous open-air fuck and was tempted, but I resolved to stick to my plan. Luke was going to suffer. Okay, the ride had thrilled me, but a plan is a plan.

I hadn't reckoned with Luke's strength and determination. He lifted me bodily and set me down on the warm seat he'd just vacated. "You drive," he said.

With his cock jutting in front of him, he mounted behind me. With one big hand on each of my hips, he lifted my ass up, tilting me forward over the handlebars. I felt him raise my skirt.

"What?" I asked.

When he pulled me down, half sitting in his lap, I understood. He'd impaled me with his hard shaft.

I wanted to protest, but it felt so *good*.

His arms reached around me. One strong hand closed over mine, on the handlebar. His other hand slipped between the buttons of my dress and found my nipple. We pulled away and back onto the road. We rode, me sitting on his lap, his leather-clad thighs beneath my naked ones. I hooked my ankles around his calves. The engine's vibrations traveled up through his cock into me. He rocked, slowly thrusting in and out of my flesh. It was the slowest fuck I'd ever enjoyed, made even better by the vibration.

When we got home, Luke tucked in and zipped up as he dismounted. I managed to clamber off, stiffly.

"So what do you think?" he asked, gloating.

"I think I'm all bruised from that ride, so I'm going to take a long, hot, scented bath. Then, when you get back . . ."

"Back?" he interrupted. "Back from where?"

"Back from closing a deal on that lovely bike." I stroked the leather seat lovingly. "And when you *do* get back, *you* are going to kiss my bruises better."

Luke burned rubber.

Morgana Baron

Mardi Gras poster: Boobs Get Beads, Big Boobs Get Big Beads, Big Bare Boobs Get Pearls.

Back to Nature

My girlfriend Suzanne and I had a day off, so I suggested a drive in the country. We had a nice lunch in a tiny town, followed by a few beers, and were back on the road by mid-afternoon, when we decided to stop by a river and soak in the cool water. Suzanne stripped down to her bra, and the water had the expected results, puckering her nipples into hard peaks. We frolicked like children, but the kisses that followed were definitely not childlike.

Horny as we were, we knew we had to head home. About halfway up a winding mountain pass, I glanced over at Suzanne, and the look on her face was unmistakable. Her shirt was undone, her bra peeking out, and her hand was lazily brushing her crotch. Her eyes were mischievous, sparkling with naughtiness. I grinned and kept watching her as I drove. She slipped a finger inside her panties and said, "You'd better find a place to pull over—now!"

About a mile farther I came to a turnout. We both ran from the Jeep. Not fifty yards away, we came across an old gray deadfall lying in the grass. Suzanne was hot, and in a hurry. I had to laugh. She got naked in record time, dropped to her knees, and braced her elbows against the log. She tossed her blond mane seductively, looked over her shoulder, and said, "Fuck me, Mitch!"

I knew she was ready, but I just had to kneel behind her and run my tongue up and down her wetness. She was sopping already.

She cried, "I need to have you in me, Mitch. Stick your tongue in, please."

I ate her wildly. Her juices were smeared all over my face. She has the best-tasting pussy I've ever eaten, and it gets wet in a heartbeat. To say she was horny would be an understatement. She bucked her hips against my face so forcefully, I was having a hard time licking her. I pulled her hips to my face and held her tightly. My tongue grazed her swollen clit. She screamed as she came.

I didn't give her a chance to recover, not that she wanted one. I got up behind her and shoved my thick cock into her. She shrieked as I rammed it home—hard!

She turned to look at me, her eyes blazing, and hissed, "That big cock was created to fuck me. Fuck me, hard, Mitch. Fuck me, now!"

My hands reached for her bouncing tits as I ground into her. I worked her nipples and then felt her hand join one of mine. God! This woman can fuck! I felt that I would lose it at any time.

Sensing it, Suzanne said, "Tell me when because I'm going to turn around and swallow it all."

That did it.

"Now!" I yelled.

She pulled away and spun around with her mouth open. I aimed at her mouth and erupted. She took it on her tongue, then leaned forward to pull my cock into her mouth. She sucked any remaining amount out of me. Then she smiled at me and I knew we weren't done.

She gave me a few minutes to recover, keeping herself busy by playing with her pussy, which was still dripping wet. I loved seeing her slide her fingers in and out. It took only a few minutes before I was hard again. She eyed my cock with a grin.

"That's what I like to see!" she said.

"Honey, you could give a dead man a hard-on," I muttered. She stood up and braced herself against a pine tree.

"Right here, right now, Mitch. Standing up against this tree!"

As I grabbed her hips, she giggled and added, "If you're a good boy, I might even let you come on my tits!"

With that vision in mind, I drove my entire length into her. She moaned, "Mmmmm . . . that's it, Mitch. Just like that. Fuck me like I'm your whore. I'm a real slut, aren't I?"

Suzanne knows how to talk dirty and she knows I love it. I could feel her pussy suck at me, almost like her mouth.

"Harder!" she screamed, and I pistoned in and out of her. I reached around, found her clit, and played with it until she went berserk.

"God, yes!" she yelled.

We fucked like animals.

"Make me come, Mitch!" she screamed. "I need to come."

Her words spurred me on. My hand left her clit and slid up to her heaving tits. Her pussy quivered, then seized around my cock. Her body shuddered in orgasm. Her come was running down my cock and down her legs.

She was exhausted, but kept her promise. She lay down on her back in the grass, looking like a goddess, and beckoned me to straddle her. I slid my penis between her gorgeous breasts. She smiled and squeezed them around my cock. I pumped, slowly at first, because I wanted to make this last.

"Fuck my tits," she urged, tossing her head back and forth. I started running my cock back and forth faster. She leaned up and licked my cockhead as it neared her face.

"Mmmmm, nice," she purred.

My hands replaced hers and I squeezed her boobs around my cock.

"Damn!" I exclaimed. "I'm close."

Her tongue kept snaking over the tip. She glanced up, waiting expectantly. Our eyes met and I told her I was going to come.

"Yes, Mitch. Now!" she yelled. I pulled back and shot a huge hot load onto her tits. She rubbed it into her nipples, then pushed some up into her mouth.

"God, you are incredible," I said.

Suzanne took my dick back into her mouth and licked me clean, then said, "Now get me home so we can do it all again."

Pilar Lopez

JennaTip #8: A Pearl of a Gift

What we're discussing here is the "pearl necklace" of ejaculate along the neckline following, in many cases, a good, hard titty-fucking.

Some people find it kinky, some disgusting, some find this an alternative to having sex when on the rag, and some find it to be a form of domination.

Sometimes he comes just from rubbing his cock between her breasts, sometimes he is getting a blow job and pulls back and comes on her tits and neck, sometimes he masturbates to orgasm and aims for her chest and neck, and sometimes he pulls out from intercourse and has such a powerful orgasm his come goes flying everywhere and by chance, according to him, reaches all the way up to her neck and breasts, but she really knows that he's aiming and trying to do it on purpose because men just are that way, by and large.

However it happens, a nice boy helps clean it up after.

The Intern

I know you won't believe that this story is true. But it is. At least most of it. I'm a thirty-eight-year-old business owner, about 6'1" tall, with lean strong muscles from my mornings out on the lake rowing. I have curly brown hair and green eyes, and my firm chin is softened by my full lips and engaging smile. Now, to the true part. I am a business owner and I'm not bad looking.

Anyway, I have about fifteen employees. Mostly they are out in the field, but I do have a couple of office workers. One is about sixty-five, has blue poodle hair, and complains about her bursitis kicking in on cool mornings. This story is not, and I am sure you'll be glad, about her. It's about my other office worker. She's an intern working on her marketing degree at the local college. She's a little older than the average student, but still pretty darn young and impressionable. She's bright, funny, talented, and even though she's really professional, there is something just so damn sexy about her it drives me nuts.

I cannot tell you how many times, after she would sit primly next to me, asking my opinion of some piece she'd written, I would have to shut and lock my office door and whack off or explode just from smelling the light, soapy scent of her shampoo. I know, I sound kind of dopey, but she really had this effect on me.

Well, this went on for about eight months. Her internship was due to end and I was going crazy at the idea of her not being there. I was moody, snapping at people, and actively avoiding her for about a week when she made an end-of-the-day appointment to talk with me about my filling out the paperwork for her professor so she could get credit.

About fifteen minutes before we were due to talk, I found myself pacing around my desk, nervous and unable to sit or think or do anything productive. I was thinking about her sitting there asking me to review her work and I was imagining how sweet she would smell. I thought about how her breasts rose with each inhale. I was thinking about how she would push her hair behind her ear, exposing her neck—making me want to bite her. I thought of how her foot would tap and jump when she was nervous or excited. I thought about all of this and I had, no surprise, a raging hard-on. I realized there was absolutely no way I could conduct a meeting in this state. I shut the door, plopped down in my chair, unzipped my fly, and pulled that big, nasty bugger out and gave in to the fantasies racing through my mind.

I imagined her kneeling there in front of me, looking up at me with those big eyes of hers, smiling sweetly and then wrapping those luscious wet lips around my cock and licking my shaft from my balls to the tip, happily tasting my dripping come.

I imagined her coming through the door and sitting down across from me with a short skirt on, crossing her legs and uncrossing her legs, giving me peeks at her wet, pink pussy. I thought about her putting her feet up on my desk, sliding her ass down in the chair, and spreading her legs and lips open for me, touching herself, pushing her fingers up inside and then licking them off as she pinched her big pink nipples.

I imagined her leaning over to pick something up and her skirt riding up to show me her gorgeous ass because she didn't have any panties on and I would be standing right behind her with my monster cock in my hand. I thought about how she'd be all wet and ready and she would lean back into me and I'd grab those amazing curves and pull her onto my hard dick, fucking her from behind as she moaned and called my name.

I was so totally gone in my fantasies of her tight wet pussy around my giant hard-on and was so close to shooting my load that I didn't realize that she really was calling my name. I moaned "yes" just as I came, and in she walked. Turns out, she'd knocked, but I hadn't heard her; she called my name, and when I said "yes" she thought I was responding to her. In my agitated state, I'd totally forgotten to lock the door.

She turned bright red, threw her hand up over her mouth, and tried to back out of the office. However, the door had swung back behind her and as she backed up, she ended up closing the door with us both still in the office. I was so shocked, I jumped up out of my seat with my rapidly waning hard-on hanging out my pants and a handful of come. She looked at me, then looked down, then up at my face again, and I thought I would die.

She didn't say anything, but she didn't leave either. She just stood there, I assumed transfixed with horror. I fell back into my chair. This certainly wasn't at all like my fantasies. In my fantasy, she'd be transfixed by lust and amazement at how enormous my cock was.

Trying to pull myself together, I grabbed a napkin from my desk drawer and wiped my hands clean. Then I straightened my tie, pulled some wrinkles out of my shirt, and nonchalantly slipped my penis back into my pants, zipping up and turning to talk to her, pretending nothing had happened.

She took a deep breath, causing those magnificent breasts to rise, walked up to the desk, leaned across, took my tie in her hand, patting it down as though to straighten it, only as her hand traveled down my chest and stomach it didn't stop at the end of the tie, but pressed against my still somewhat hard cock. She looked me right in the eyes, holding me there, making me look at her, gave my package a squeeze, smiled, and said "Impressive display, sir. Perhaps we should discuss whether you would like to hire me on part-time, as it seems there's so much more I can learn from you than was apparent."

She licked her lips, removed her hand, crossed the room, with a heart-stopping sway in her hips, glanced back over her shoulder as she went through the door, winking at me and blowing me a kiss.

Needless to say, she got a rave review from me for her school, a part-time job offer, and we've been actively exploring what I can teach her. I tell you this, though, turns out, she's one hell of an instructor in her own right.

Darren Reese

My Babysitter

My husband sometimes wakes me up with his fingers well up my pussy and his hard cock pushing into the small of my back, telling me he has to fuck me. I'll roll over and help him inside me and about this time is when he wakes up. I swear. He sleep-fucks. I thought he was just screwing around when he would accuse me later of molesting him and attacking him while he was asleep, because he's always the one to initiate these middle-of-the-night fuck-fests, but it turns out that this isn't unique to him. Other people do it.

I tried to imagine a way to use this to my advantage. Eventually, I did.

I've had this recurring fantasy that I use to get off when I masturbate. I have never told my husband about it because it involves him. Anyway, the way I finally used his sleep-fucking was to get my fantasy fulfilled.

See, I fantasize about watching my husband fuck another woman. I don't want to tell him about it because I don't want him out there picking out women to fuck. I want to decide the woman, when, where, etc. I want it to be up to me and I worried that if I told him about it, he'd be so gung-ho that I'd actually get all jealous and resentful and then that would completely ruin my fantasy. This is, after all, supposed to be all about getting me off.

Additionally, my fantasy isn't just about any other woman. It isn't about a friend or anything like that. I fantasize about my husband being with a young virgin, someone just out of college, like a babysitter. But I don't want it to actually be our babysitter. That would just be too strange. That's the fantasy part.

Getting back to the story, what I did was I arranged a "new" babysitter. I actually called an escort service from the paper and met with several young women to pick just the right one. She was about twenty-three but could pass for nineteen or twenty. She wasn't a virgin, by any means, but she did have this innocent look to her with her long straight hair pulled back in a headband and her demure outfit. She had these big brown eyes and trim little body. She was perfect.

We made our arrangements and then I set up an elaborate evening out that would go really late. I told my husband that our regular babysitter wasn't available, but she had recommended this new person and since we were going to be out really late I had asked the sitter to stay over and not worry about trying to stay up and then drive home, and she agreed. He fell for it hook, line, and sinker.

Of course, my regular sitter actually came to watch the kids, arriving just after we left and leaving a little before we got home. I told her the escort was a niece.

So our evening out included me dressing really, really sexy in a backless, silky top without a bra so my nipples brushed the fabric and stayed rock-hard for everyone to see all night long, a pair of black leather pants that hugged my ass and curvy hips perfectly, showing off my firm body, and a pair of tall heels with pointy toes and little straps that circled my ankles, showing off my petite feet.

We went to listen to some jazz and have drinks, then ate a fabulous seafood dinner, before heading to a club for some dancing. I was teasing my husband mercilessly, rubbing against him, kissing him, asking him if he liked my breasts or wanted to feel me up. I had him going and good.

I was doing this because I have learned that the way to instigate these sleep-fucks is to get him all ready and horny, talk dirty to him, kiss him, and rub against him, and then go to sleep without letting him let off steam, so to speak.

It was around 2 A.M. when we finally got home. The babysitter was sitting on the couch, just as I instructed, in a short little cotton nightie that barely covered her. She looked adorable, hot, sexy, young, and just like what I imagined. My husband was staring and trying not to drool. He had no idea what I was up to and that was the way I wanted it. I had her dress like that and turn him on because that's my fantasy.

I teased him in the bedroom about how he wanted her and wanted to fuck her. I said I thought she was probably a virgin and seemed a little naive. This just got him more aroused and frustrated when after a little light petting, I said I was just too tired, rolled over, and pretended to go to sleep.

I knew he was really tired and had had enough to drink that he probably wouldn't just finish himself off and he didn't. He grumbled a little, then started to snore as he fell asleep.

I went to the living room to get the fake sitter. We talked a little bit more about what I wanted done, then I led her to our bedroom. I helped her slide onto the bed, then we carefully lifted the covers off so that I would have an unobstructed view of what happened. Also, I had out the video camera to catch it all on film and didn't want to miss anything.

I leaned across her and kissed my husband on the ear, then pulled away as she spooned up against him, putting her arm around him and caressing first his thigh and then trailing a finger along his rapidly hardening cock.

It didn't take long at all before he rolled over and started pawing at her body. He went straight for her wet pussy, sticking first one, then two fingers in her. He started rubbing up against her hip and thigh with his hard cock. He started begging her to let him fuck her. All the time he did this, his eyes were completely closed and I knew he was still asleep. I didn't know how this would work out if he woke up, which he usually does, but I had told the girl to try to fuck him but keep him asleep. Not an easy task, but she was up for it, and it looked like he was up for anything with that big hard cock of his.

I was so horny I was glad the video camera was on a stand because I was touching myself, pulling my nipples and caressing my own pussy and clit, totally getting off to my husband grabbing and touching this other young woman. The fact that she was "playing" the babysitter just made it that much sweeter to me.

She rolled over so her back was to him and lifted up her ass against him. He pulled his fingers from her pussy and started fingering her ass and pushing his thumb in. He asked her to suck his cock, so she rolled around again and went down on him, tonguing and licking his head, sucking his pre-come. She climbed up into a 69 position and lowered her pussy to his face and in his sleep he ate her, sticking his tongue up into her pussy and her ass and then circling her clit. She came right there on his face and he slept through the whole thing.

Because I was worried that he would wake up when he came, I had her switch places with me as she flipped back around from sucking his cock. I was so hot and wet and had already come once just watching. I slipped into the bed next to him and pulled him over on top of me. He rammed that giant cock of his home, fucking me like the world was ending, talking dirty and telling me what he wanted to do to me, first fucking me while I was on my knees, then sliding his cock up my ass. He was really hot and ready to go and I knew neither one of us would last much longer.

Suddenly his eyes flew open, he threw his head back, and

slammed down hard into me coming with giant heaves and spurts. I felt his cock pulsing and that pushed me over the edge so that I came, too. The girl stayed out of his view and finished taping, then silently let herself out. I held him until he fell back into a deep sleep, then got up, put the camera away, and covered us back up with the comforter, cuddling up to him for the rest of the night.

In the morning, thinking I had pulled one off, we had a late breakfast with the "sitter." Just as she was leaving, my husband stopped her and asked her if she was available to come again for us and from the way he said it, I realized he hadn't been asleep the whole time at all.

She winked and left and then he and I went up to the bedroom because he really wanted to see the tape. I cannot say I am disappointed that he figured it out and was on to us. We have, in fact, had that sitter over again. This time she fulfilled a fantasy of his. Turns out he often jacked off to imagining me with the young babysitter. Who am I to leave a fantasy unfulfilled?

Francis Underwood

JennaTip #9: Unconscious Desires

Sleep-fucking (sleepsex, sexsomnia, SBS) is not so very different from sleepwalking except that it relates entirely to sexual behavior that occurs during sleep. You've likely heard stories about someone's younger brother walking in his sleep and ending up downstairs pissing in the corner of the living room before walking right back up to bed and never remembering a thing. Sleepsex is not all that different, except of course it shouldn't be your friend's younger brother unless he's an adult and so are you, and generally it isn't the sort of story you share at family dinners.

Lots of people masturbate while asleep. Lots of people will deny masturbating while asleep. They also deny snoring.

Sometimes the sleeper awakens only to deny initiating the sex. Sometimes the sleeper doesn't wake at all, though that's not nearly as much fun (probably).

Sleepsex causes problems when it is misunderstood. It is not a conscious act, but an unconscious or subconscious act, and blaming a sleeper for masturbating or groping and trying to initiate sex while asleep is tantamount to yelling at the little brother who peed in the corner. Unless the sleepsexer has a habit of sleeping platonically in the same bed with other people, it shouldn't create much of a problem as long as the partner understands what is happening and doesn't take offense, get angry, find fault, or any of the other myriad things that might very well happen because unfortunately too many people are all tied up in knots, and not in a good way, about sex.

If you know a sleepsexer and you are concerned or they are, there is a book (*Sleepsex: Uncovered*) about people who are sexsomniacs, which may help explain the causes and could allay most concerns.

Out of the Blue

I hadn't seen Marian for at least five years. Once we graduated from university we went our separate ways. So it was a pleasant surprise to receive a call from her out of the blue. In no time, we regressed to our sophomoric selves and were giggling like idiots. When she said she was coming to town for a conference, I insisted she stay an extra night and spend it with Jeff and me. She readily agreed.

Believe it or not, I didn't even recall our girlish college experimenting, sexually, until I was off the phone. Maybe it was buried in my subconscious, or maybe it was so much a part of my past that it didn't register right away, and by the time it did, it was too late.

Jeff was working that night, making overtime dollars to spend on our upcoming wedding. It was just Marian and me for dinner. For some reason it took me a long time to get ready. My pink knit dress was clingy, with a V-neck that probably was a little low for a dinner date with a girlfriend. I almost changed but in the end decided it'd be okay to show off a bit.

When I opened the door, I saw that Marian had dressed up, too. Her little black satin dress had spaghetti straps and an even shorter skirt than mine. She was wearing sheer black hose. Her shoes were dressy, black pumps with serious heels. She's tinier than me, dark and arty, while I'm a ditzy blonde.

We stared at each other in the doorway for a moment. Neither of us had changed much. We threw our arms around each other and hugged hard. The physical memories flooded through me, shocking me at how I responded to the feel of her in my arms. I guess I'd forgotten how much I'd loved her.

Possibly we drank more wine than was appropriate for dinner, or maybe it was reliving the past with my best friend from my youth, but I was giddy by the time we settled in front of the fireplace, with Cointreau and coffee handy. We were both on the couch, twisted toward each other, my legs curled beneath me, my knee just touching her thigh where the slit in her skirt fell open to bare her thigh-high tops. I had to wonder what she'd had in mind as she dressed. Seriously, who wears dark, sheer thigh-high stockings with delicate lacy tops for a night out with the girls?

"Tell me all about your fiancé," she said.

I was more than happy to comply.

When I was finished, she said, "I can't wait to meet him. He sounds like a dream come true. Tall, dark, and handsome."

"He's perfect," I said.

"I don't know if I could do it," she mused, "commit to one man for the rest of my life. That's a lot of time with the same partner, even if he is gorgeous."

"I love him. Plus, he's a dynamo in bed," I boasted.

"Sure, but your motto was, 'Variety keeps life spicy.'"

"That was a long time ago," I protested, though I was grinning. "I hope you'll keep that tidbit to yourself!"

We were silent for a moment, then our eyes met and we burst into simultaneous giggles.

"Remember how in love we were?" She raised an eyebrow at me.

"Don't even go there!" I held up my hand, but she ignored me.

"All of a sudden we had this huge crush on each other. Don't tell me you don't remember!"

"Of course I do," I said. "How could I forget? Passing notes to each other in Comp. Lit."

"Canceling dates so we could be together."

"You gave me a beaded bracelet. I still have it," I said.

"I don't believe you!"

"Come on," I replied. I led her to the bedroom.

I was in the walk-in closet for a while, unearthing my box of mementoes, so I didn't know what she was doing until I emerged, box in hand. The sneaky little she-beast had found my dress-up drawer! My feather boa was around her neck and she was holding my silver dolphin vibrator.

"Does this thing work as well as they say?"

"I forgot what a snoop you are," I grumbled.

She vamped, letting the boa slide down her arm. The spaghetti strap of her little black dress fell off her shoulder with it. "Let's play," she said. She switched the vibrator on, then off again, quickly, before I had a chance to protest. "It'll be fuuuun."

I didn't know what to say, so I opened the box and found the bracelet. "See?"

She took it from me. "It was supposed to be a symbol of our eternal Sapphic love," she said, turning the bracelet in her hand. "Who knew it would fade so quickly?"

"Those were wild times, but it's all in the past now," I replied.

She took the bracelet from me. "Hold out your hand," she ordered.

Marian moved closer, so close I could smell her musk beneath the floral scent she wore. She took her time, stroking my wrist with her delicate fingers. Each little caress sent shivers up my spine. When she was done, she put my hand on her hip, wrapped her arms around my neck and kissed me.

I'd forgotten the particular sensation of kissing a woman— this woman, as I'd never kissed another. Her lips were lush, soft on soft. Her tongue was nimble, delicate, flicking against my teeth until I opened my mouth and welcomed it inside. Our tongues danced, delighted to be reunited. I fell into the kiss. I wanted it to last forever, partly because it was so thrilling and partly because I intended to nip this experience in the bud.

Marian cupped my left breast. My nipple ached to be rubbed, even pinched between two of her elegantly manicured fingers. Of course I was wearing a bra, but it was just a satiny little thing. Her hand easily found my hardening nipple. It was almost a relief, for a moment, when she captured it and urged it to stiffness. But when she stopped kissing my mouth and started kissing her way down my throat toward the V in the neck of my dress, I found my voice.

"Marian, I can't."

She looked up at me with her gorgeous chocolate eyes. I remembered that her nipples were almost the same color, and how lucky I'd felt, once, to know that. "I can't cheat on Jeff."

"Silly," she murmured, her voice husky, the way it gets when she's horny. "I'd never make you choose between me and your man." She straightened, releasing my breast.

Why, I wondered, did I feel so disappointed to have my words respected? Marian turned back to my dress-up drawer. When she turned back she was wearing the cap of my vinyl "lady-cop" outfit.

"Up against the wall, doll. Or I'll shoot!" She pointed my plastic revolver-vibrator at me.

I put my hands up, but otherwise I didn't move. "You can't make me, hon."

"Oh, yeah?" She squeezed the trigger. The vibrator hummed. Our eyes met and we both burst into laughter. "Don't make me shoot again!" She waved her weapon.

"I'll do whatever you say, officer," I purred. "Only please don't shoot me."

She tilted the brim of the cap to a jaunty angle. "That's more like it. Lie down on the bed."

Neither of us was laughing, anymore.

A sexual romp can play tricks with time. I'd noticed that before and I noticed it that night. It seemed like only minutes had passed before Jeff came home, but they were such wild, sexy minutes and those playful minutes must have added up to at least an hour, otherwise we never could have accomplished all the crazy, hot things we did. Anyway, Jeff came home and I found that it was suddenly much later than I thought.

"Hello?" His voice betrayed his eagerness to meet my friend. Surprise, too, at finding the house seemingly empty.

"We're in here!" Marian called out. I wasn't able to speak.

"What're you doing in . . ." Jeff didn't finish the sentence. He didn't have to. It was pretty obvious what we were up to.

I was spread-eagled, naked, my wrists and ankles tied to the four bedposts by silk scarves. Another silk scarf served as my gag, thus I was unable to speak. My body glistened from the oil Marian had rubbed all over me. My pussy glistened too, wet with my desire and Marian's saliva.

"Patricia's been a bad girl," purred Marion. She'd taken her satin dress off and put the lady-cop accessories, including badge and holster, on. Now that I was restrained she no longer had to keep me covered, so the gun was back in its holster. She looked amazing. "I'm afraid she's in need of discipline."

"I see, I guess." Jeff looked embarrassed, but there was tension in his voice. "Did you forget I was coming home?"

"Not at all," she replied, twirling a nightstick. "We've been waiting for you."

"Oh," he said.

I started to panic. Had I gambled my entire future on an act of passion? This wasn't college anymore. I was supposed to be an adult now.

Marian bent over the dress-up drawer, granting Jeff a generous glimpse of her bottom, bare except for a slip of silk thong between her cheeks. When she stood she held the crop, which she offered to him.

"I believe you have experience in disciplining Patricia?"

"Oh." He took the crop.

"She's confessed to a passion for nipple torture, and I'm afraid I'm not adept enough with the crop to give her what she craves."

His eyes met mine. A slow, sexy smile crossed his lips. "I get it."

I relaxed. He did get it—and now it was my turn to get it.

We played all night long. They tortured me for a while, but after I came nicely for them, they let me go. I licked Marian's pussy. I made her come like that.

Jeff's orgasm was intense. When it was over, Marian asked if we'd killed him. When he opened his eyes, they were glazed with pleasure.

Later, we fucked like animals. I don't know if our passion was ever truly spent or if we were eventually just too exhausted to go on. We fell asleep, three in a bed, with me in the middle.

Marcy Rosewood

JennaTip #10: LUG Love

To be a Lesbian Until Graduation (LUG) is to suggest that a woman chooses to engage in sexual activity with other women not because of any biological drive but because it is a current lifestyle choice. The concept that sexual orientation is more fluid in women than in men has found support in various studies, conducted in Los Angeles by men, of course. That's not entirely true. Women have found the same results and not only in Los Angeles.

These findings suggest that contrary to our cultural model of sexual identity, the choice of romantic partner and interest for some women is just that, a choice.

Not all people believe that sexual identity is a choice and for some people, apparently it isn't, but studies repeatedly have supported the idea that women do not have the same biological drive as men when it comes to sexual identity. Those who disagree with the studies feel that LUGs are experimenting and have determined to try on lesbianism to avoid unwanted male attention, to have undisturbed focus on their studies, to avoid the mistakes of an unwanted pregnancy or a too-early marriage due to making the mistake of *falling in love* with a man while still in school.

Whatever the reason, bisexuality among young women does appear to be gaining in popularity whether as a fad or because women have more freedom to pursue their desires in today's world than the past, at least in the United States. In other countries, women have been encouraged to find sexual satisfaction and companionship with one another, particularly in cultures that allow for multiple wives, as the husband cannot be attentive to all his wives all the time and does not want another man to fill that need. This is just a tidbit of a JennaTip, however, and not a dissertation, so we'll end here, but this topic could easily fill an entire book or two.

Makes me wish I lived somewhere with public transit.

The Subway

No one could understand. How could they? I don't even understand myself. I never dreamed I could actually do anything like this. Well, maybe I dreamed it, but I always thought my fantasies would stay fantasies. I'm still in shock. I just couldn't stop myself. Or him.

I feel ready to burst and don't know whom to trust, but I have to tell someone.

What happened is, I was coming home from work—it was about 5:30. I ride the subway. There were about a hundred people in the car. Personal space was nonexistent, elbows digging into my side, briefcases banging my shins, no movement of the tired and stale air.

So, on this trip, I was pleasantly surprised to inhale a strong masculine aftershave as I wedged myself into the wall of riders. I turned my head slightly. The scent came from the man directly on my left. Streaks of silver jetted through his black hair. Exquisitely dressed, he radiated power. All in all, he was rather intoxicating.

He caught me looking and his lips curved into a smile, revealing a row of startlingly white teeth. I turned quickly and looked out the window at the rushing darkness. I caught my own reflection in the window. My long dark hair was wavy from the humidity and my skin seemed to glow. Then I caught his reflection. He still smiled. My chest rose and fell noticeably as I took a nervous intake of air. He was watching me.

Part of me wanted him intensely.

The other part only wanted him a lot.

As we sped through a tunnel, it happened. The car jerked and

I suddenly felt something pressing against the back of my hand. I tried to push away whatever it was, when I suddenly realized what I was pushing against. I drew in a sharp breath and glanced up. The man was smiling at me with the same upturned lips. I was in shock. I didn't know what to do. Then I realized he was still pressing his stiff member against my hand, and I raised my arm abruptly and shifted my body away. I felt both revulsion and excitement.

Without knowing it, I had now placed myself directly before him. Another jerk of the subway train, and suddenly I felt him pressing against my behind. I stood still in disbelief as he stayed right there, not moving away, but firmly pressed against me.

I was going to say something, but my nerve failed me. In all honesty, I hadn't been this close to any man for a long time, much less one so deliriously attractive. It also felt good to have a man's body pressing against mine, even a stranger's, even in a subway. It was undeniably stimulating. With each jerk of the subway car, I felt him press deeper. I told myself I could leave at any moment, but I was getting aroused, and I remained standing where I was. I felt guilty about what I was doing. But then I figured it happens all the time at dance clubs. Besides, what could I really do? There was barely enough room to breathe, let alone move anywhere.

At the next station the subway car screeched to a stop, and as the riders began moving out to the platform, a low voice whispered in my ear. "Next time wear a skirt."

I turned my head, but no one was there. The stranger had already stepped out of the car and was disappearing among the milling crowd on the platform.

That night I lay in bed, thinking about the handsome stranger. I couldn't believe his nerve! To push himself against me and then tell me to wear a skirt the next time! Who did he think he was? There was not going to be any "next time"!

Yet, I had to admit I was fiercely attracted to him. I wasn't even so annoyed by his arrogance as by his getting me so hot and then abandoning me.

The next morning, I deliberately put on pants. Two could play this game of erotic frustration.

Better yet, I thought, and went back to my bedroom and threw open my closet. I pushed aside racks of clothes. I knew what I was looking for—a skirt and not just a skirt, a miniskirt to slip into after work.

Maybe.

Just in case.

I could wear it to taunt the arrogant stranger. I wanted to frustrate the hell out of him.

At the end of work, I went to the bathroom and slipped out of my pants and into the bit of cloth that passed for a skirt. I wanted the handsome stranger to get just as hot and bothered as he had gotten me, and then I'd abandon him just as abruptly. I entered the same subway car at 5:30. I glanced around. He wasn't there. I felt a measure of disappointment, mixed with relief. Then I saw him in the rear-door window of the next car. He was smiling at me.

At the next station he walked down the platform and pushed his way into my car. He was wearing a dark suit with a crisp white shirt and silk tie of deep blue. He worked his way over to me, and at the sight of my miniskirt, gave a curt nod of approval. I flushed at his thinking I really was wearing it for him, when I was wearing it as revenge.

Before I knew it, he had maneuvered himself behind me. I could smell his aftershave once again. A sudden jerk of the car, and I felt his stiff cock press into me. I wanted to pull away, but as my heart pounded in my ears, I felt powerless to do anything.

The subway car clattered and screeched as it went around a corner. I felt him step back with relief. I took a half step forward, but another jerk of the car threw me against him, and this time I felt his hand clamp onto my hip. His voice came soft and low in my ear: "Careful now, or you'll hurt yourself." His hand remained on my hip.

His grip was strong. Here was an audacious man who was unafraid when it came to taking what he wanted.

My skirt lifted suddenly and I felt the back of his hand brush against my left cheek. His hand turned over, and I felt him massage my cheek with his fingertips, then he grasped it firmly. I wanted to cry out, but no words could escape my mouth.

I suddenly felt his index finger slowly slip down to right between my legs. Lightly he stroked his finger over the fabric of my panties. I gasped, but no one seemed to notice. The subway picked up speed as he continued to stroke me with the tip of his finger, back and forth. Unable to stifle myself any longer, I let out a small moan.

"Shhh. Quiet now," he whispered in my ear.

I thought he might leave me right then again, but he wasn't finished yet. He worked his finger underneath my panties, and—with one swift gesture—slipped it all the way inside me. Keeping his finger there, he tormented me by not moving it at all. I found myself gently rocking my hips. Between the rocking of my hips and the rocking of the subway car, I felt I was going to explode.

Just when I thought I couldn't take it anymore, I felt a second finger of his slide inside. I bit down on my lip, trying to silence my groans of pleasure. With the first wave of orgasm, a shudder coursed through me, flying up my spine, causing a soft sigh to escape my mouth.

One woman, a few feet away, looked at me, but at that point I didn't care if anyone noticed. I was leaning my whole body into the handsome stranger, and with the slow rocking of the subway, I slowly built to my second orgasm. Just when I was on the brink, he withdrew both his fingers and whispered in my ear, "Tomorrow, skirt, but no panties."

I know I shouldn't meet him tomorrow, no matter how handsome and compelling. But I'm sitting here naked, setting out my outfit for tomorrow. I've picked out a skirt, not pants. It's on my chair with my bra and blouse. Beneath the chair, are my shoes. I've forgotten my panties.

I wonder if in the morning they'll remain forgotten. I wonder if I'll get on the same subway car again. I wonder.

J. P. West

Oh, I love, I love, I love my little Calendar Man.

Mr. February

Jake, a sweet-looking hottie of a cocktail waitress, was perusing the available likelies at a new spot in town, at least new to him. He was in the mood for a little something sweet and raw. And he saw it at the club, on the dance floor, in dark jeans that were plenty baggy, though not so baggy the giant cock that was wearing them couldn't be seen, at least the outline of it.

Jake has moves and his current move du jour was to purchase two drinks, one for himself and one for the object of his obsession. This night he ordered a scotch and soda and a martini, hoping *mister most likely* liked martinis.

And that is when it happened. Jake, with hooded eyes and chiseled jaw, was making his way through the crowd, drinks in hand, when a woman approached his target, kissed him with tongue, and immediately Jake thinks he's been had by another fucking fag stag, straight but liking the groove of the gay bar.

Jake turns, frustrated, downs the scotch and prepares to sip the martini, hoping he won't have a deadly headache or worse in the morning, but before he's turned completely, the long, tall tease makes eye contact, direct eye contact, and winks with his traffic-stopping blue eye unmatched in this world, Jake thinks, except by the other one next to it.

With a nonchalant toss of his head, he speaks volumes to Jake. *Stop. Don't go another step. Turn and wait over there. Yes, by the hall. Yes, you. Yes.*

Jake does. He watches as his quarry now turned hunter whispers something to the woman, then walks his way. He walks decisively through the crowd and with little more than a raise of his eyebrow and a twitch of a smile, he walks past Jake and Jake follows like a moon orbits a planet.

Jake follows him down the hall and into the bathroom. The empty bathroom. It was early yet, at least for this club, though a bit surprising to find it vacant.

Leaning against the door, Jake's new friend smiles and with his husky voice teases out a "Hello" followed by instructions. "Help me put down some paper towels for my knees, now lower your pants and pull out your cock. I'm straight but on the down low and I love cock, I really love it, the taste and the smell, but my girlfriend will wonder if this takes too long and wow, that is really long. So let's get started here, if you don't mind."

And Jake, as if in a trance, mesmerized by this lovely man kneeling now before him, does as he's told.

He tells Jake, "No, this is not my first time. In fact, this is a monthly thing. I would do it more often but I can only convince my girlfriend to come for the monthly drag contest, which will be much later, so I only get to suck cock once a month and I have to hurry, sorry, but don't worry, it'll be great and thank you for coming in here with me."

He tongues Jake's cock, he sticks his tongue into Jake's little slit at the top of his head. He looks up and tells Jake, "Yes, I'm very good at this. It'll be quick but it'll be memorable. I promise."

And he is. He is fucking good at cocksucking. He's really into it, moaning and pulling and whimpering. Jake is unable to talk and unable to move. All he can do is look down at the curly dark hair, the razor-sharp cheekbones, the broad shoulders, and the occasional tip of a pink tongue and try not to come immediately.

He mouths Jake's balls and licks up the length of his cock. Jake notices he can see a little of this in the mirror over the sink, Jake is about to come when . . .

"Get your stupid, fucking, cock-sucking, cheating, dumb-fuck, fucking ass out of the bathroom." The girlfriend has a really powerful voice. She's hammering on the door. Kicking it, trying to force it open, but the guy is kneeling so his feet are against the door and it doesn't budge.

"I am so fucking tired of you sneaking off to suck dick, you little shitbag. I hate you." She sounds very, very angry. Not sad. Not upset. Angry. Actually beat-you-to-death-with-a-hammer angry. Jake's not angry. He's scared. He tries to pull away, but the guy digs his fingers into Jake's thighs. He holds him against his face. He sucks and pulls and despite himself, Jake comes in great gushes, which are swallowed as his conquistador stands, straightens his shirt that was barely rumpled, and before Jake has moved, unlocks and opens the door.

Jake stands there, dick hanging out, and there is a crowd of men all looking in, all waiting for this exact moment to happen. Jake yanks his pants up, pushing his cock back through the fly, and tries to slip out unnoticed, which is an impossible feat in a narrow hallway with twenty or thirty men all standing and watching his every move.

As Jake walks off he hears someone yell. "Check it out, here comes Mr. February."

Jake stalks through the club's doors to the sounds of cheering and the flash of a camera.

The bar fundraiser is always a giant success, though the calendars are sold only to a small group of high-paying patrons, including, of course, the owner, with his curly dark hair, broad shoulders, and unbelievably blue eyes.

Sean Dougherty

Ding! Big, hard, wet dong! This story certainly did ring my bell.

Being Inside

Mark had teased her about finding the kind of bar in San Francisco that made the city famous; a place where sexual preference was irrelevant, gender was mutable, and public displays of everything short of fornication were common.

They settled for Café du Nord, a hip, slightly rundown establishment furnished and lit by more than enough bordello red. The patrons ranged from shy geeks to outrageous performers, but the atmosphere held enough mystery to keep Mark and Elaine there for several drinks.

The tables varied in size, and each had its own arrangement of (formerly) plush seating. As the couple snuggled in a faded rouge Victorian settee, Mark whispered into her hair.

"Check out Miss Blue and Melancholy over there." He tried to nod in the woman's general direction but with Elaine behind him, it took her a few minutes to figure out which woman he meant. When she located the subject of his remarks, though, she knew exactly what he referred to and giggled. The blonde with two wispy streaks of blue to frame her pretty but painted face pouted on her perch at the bar. She caught Mark and Elaine looking at her, but instead of turning away, she held the gaze and let her mouth slide into a mischievous grin.

"Oh, now you've done it," Mark teased. "She's noticed us."

"I think she's just noticed you."

"Well, in any event, we're about to get a visitation."

The odd but intriguing woman approached. The slow, studied sway of her walk accentuated the cinched bustier's affect on her slim waist and rounded hips. Her tits nestled firmly into the cups of the garment but with every step she took, they jiggled just enough to communicate their preference for freedom. Hollywood would have considered her overweight, but Elaine knew that Mark would find her on the tasty side of luscious. Elaine was surprised to note she shared that opinion.

The woman, who finally arrived after a breathtaking but nearly interminable saunter toward them, raised her eyebrows and pointed to the settee. There was room for one more body, so Mark gestured that she should sit next to Elaine.

Up close, the woman's skin—from décolletage to hairline— had a dewy, delicate quality that contrasted sharply, almost comically, with the heavy kohl of her eye makeup. She was Heidi in Transylvania. Despite the jarring streaks of blue in her hair and the burgundy slash of color at her mouth, there was a disarming sweetness about her. Her age was hard to pinpoint—Elaine guessed somewhere in her early twenties.

Mark's arms were still wrapped around Elaine as she leaned back into his warm chest, which had become decidedly warmer with the arrival of the Goth angel. He extended a hand to the woman, probably to elicit words from her, but also because he was an outgoing kind of guy.

"Hi, I'm Mark, and this is Elaine."

She smiled, thereby subtracting yet another five years from her apparent age. "Gervais. I think you don't live in San Francisco."

They laughed politely, even though the comment irritated Elaine. What was Gervais trying to say? That they looked like hicks or something?

"No, we're here from Lake City."

"I could tell because you look too happy."

"Well, we are," Elaine agreed, relieved that her assumption about Gervais had been wrong.

"I love that. It really turns me on." Gervais's big blue eyes—a disconcerting visual echo of the stripes in her hair—widened earnestly. Her breasts heaved slightly and Elaine couldn't help but watch them reassert themselves back into place when the sigh had passed.

"Do you like big tits?" Gervais's head tilted and she awaited a response from either Mark or Elaine or both.

"Yes," they answered in unison, laughing at their timing.

"I'm glad. I like them, too. Yours are nice," she nodded at Elaine's formidable pair. Elaine blushed, more out of pride than embarrassment. "I have a dildo in my bag. Wouldn't it be fun to use it?"

Elaine decided to leave this one up to Mark. They'd often talked about a threesome. Well, more of a slave situation, really, but Gervais seemed a far cry from a dominatrix, so perhaps this was the opportunity they'd been waiting for.

He turned around to look directly at Elaine. The bar's red lights and furnishings cast rich depth to his brown hair and eyes and made his tanned skin appear darker. She read his interest as well as his caution. The angle of his eyebrows told her he needed her encouragement.

"I think we have time, don't we, honey?" Elaine asked.

Gervais led them to a third-floor walk-up about two blocks away in the Castro neighborhood. Like its owner, the flat spoke of fairy tales, death, sprites, and crucifixes. Turquoise, heart-shaped pillows were strewn below an Edward Gorey print, while a tarantula sat patiently in its terrarium. A Britney Spears compact disc lay on the stereo. Elaine imagined Gervais's underwear—days of the week scrawled in blood.

Gervais took her time lighting candles. As she moved about the room, she told the couple they could get naked if they wanted to.

"As soon as I'm finished here, I'd really like to fuck you both up the ass," she said, as if announcing what ride she planned to enjoy next at Disneyland.

Mark and Elaine undressed themselves down to underclothes. The cool San Francisco night floated through the room, chilling Elaine slightly. She looked over at Mark, whose erection was as stiff as her nipples.

"Oh!" Gervais exclaimed when she noticed Mark's bulge. "Won't you take those off so I can see you?"

Mark glanced at Elaine, who nodded and grinned. He stepped out of his briefs quickly, revealing all eight glorious inches of compliance.

"And I know you don't want to hide those pretty titties," she smiled at Elaine, who instantly unhooked her bra and flung it off happily.

Gervais unsnapped her skirt and waited for it to whoosh to the floor at her feet. Then, she kicked the garment aside and knelt before Mark. She didn't attempt to remove the bustier. With no fanfare but surprising concentration, she swooped down on his cock. He nearly teetered at the sudden intensity of her sucking.

From where Elaine stood in tingling awe, the finesse with which Gervais made Mark's cock disappear and reappear again between her dark lips was uncannily like the method Elaine herself used on him. How did this woman know exactly what he liked? Come to think of it, how did she know they would respond positively to her invitation to anal play?

Mark's groans interrupted her musings. As Gervais sucked, he thrust himself in and out of her mouth, fucking it in long, deep motions. Seeing him abandon himself to this stranger stirred something in Elaine and emboldened her to step toward Gervais and stand next to her with her legs in a wide-open V.

Maybe Gervais caught her scent. Maybe she couldn't resist unencumbered pussy. Elaine willed the young woman's hand to her creaming lips and in seconds, that's exactly where they were. Gervais diddled Elaine as she sucked Mark. The couple watched each other's arousal catapult to a fever pitch—they'd never seen wild-eyed horniness in one another caused by a third party.

Elaine desperately searched for something to grasp as the throbbing pulse between her legs intensified and rendered her knees useless. Gervais's shoulder was closest. The moment she clutched it was the moment the tremors claimed her body. Her shouts filled the room and even as she collapsed in stages beside Gervais, her orgasm persisted, twitching and twisting its way to a close. Gervais instinctively moved her hand from Elaine's cunt to her asshole, spreading the juices from one hole to the other. After several applications of Elaine's own natural lubricant, Gervais's finger rimmed her asshole, causing Elaine to position herself on all fours. Her face was inches from the carpet, which smelled of patchouli and wet dog.

"Prepare to get fucked," Gervais said.

Elaine had her back to them, but knew that if Gervais could speak, she was no longer eating Mark. So, when his thickness pushed at her ready hole, she grinned and winced with a new wave of pleasure. While he inserted himself past her forgiving sphincter, Gervais got up and stood before Elaine and Mark. The couple fucked and watched Gervais strap on the aforementioned dildo, which was the same shade of hellish red as her lipstick.

But she was watching them, too, and with every penetration, she stroked her dildo as if it were her very own cock. Her eyes glistened with ethereal delight. Her breathing was shorter, like a man's would be as his balls tightened with excitement.

"How can I help you?" she rasped. The submission in her voice came out in a plaintive purr.

"Fuck me in the ass, like you promised," Mark blurted out.

Elaine couldn't remember who moved whom in what position, but she found herself on her back, with Mark now entering her pussy. Her big tits bumped and jiggled as she absorbed his pounding.

Out of the corner of her eye, she saw Gervais get behind Mark, where the man's body now obscured her movements. A minute or so passed, during which he pumped Elaine's pussy, ramming himself so deeply inside her that he nearly tickled her spine.

But she knew when Gervais's dildo poked its way into his hole. He paused, bit his lip, shut his eyes, and stifled a high groan. Once Gervais was in—and fucking—he resumed his pumping, matching Gervais's rhythm. He'd slam into Elaine, Gervais would slam into him. Damp skin met and slid against damp skin. Squishing, slippery noises sputtered throughout.

His abdomen tensed and his posture changed. Suddenly, his shoulders were larger. His chest rippled with muscles Elaine had never noticed before. Gervais's little grunts punctuated every new push up his ass. Elaine knew he was close.

He roared when he came, but the sound was nothing compared to the colossal pounding he directed into Elaine's pussy. He trembled with demonic fervor, and seemed to want to pass that fervor along to his wife. Or was it too much for him to contain and he *had* to share it, else it destroy him?

Elaine came, too, but the intensity of his orgasm blurred with her own and she couldn't distinguish which pulses emanated from him, and which from her.

Gervais extracted herself from Mark slowly and got to her feet. She walked out of the room while her guests let earthly concerns gradually invade their thoughts. After several minutes, Gervais returned, smiling, still wearing only her bustier.

"Take your time recovering. I think I'll just go to bed now, if you don't mind. Just go ahead and let yourselves out when you're ready."

Mark's eyes darkened. He looked like he wanted to say something, but didn't know how. Gervais recognized his hesitation and asked him if everything was all right.

"Oh, yes. Everything is fantastic," he replied. "But, I was, uh, wondering . . . Do we need to leave you any money?"

Elaine hadn't considered the possibility that Gervais did this for a living. Or a supplement to a living. She hoped Mark's question wouldn't offend her.

Gervais smiled. "No, I don't do this for money."

Though her answer seemed to satisfy Mark, now it was Elaine who was curious. Gervais hadn't come at all during the night, which made her voluntary participation all the more mysterious. What was in it for this strange woman with the tarantula roommate?

"So, why do you do it?" Elaine ventured.

A beatific grin spread across the semi-Goth girl's smeared lipsticked face. "There are very few lovers out in the world," she said quietly, zipping up her skirt. "They are so rare—like endangered species. When I see people who are happy, I want to experience that happiness, know that kind of love. When I saw the two of you, I knew I could not only fulfill some of your fantasies, but satisfy my own need for ecstasy, even for a few seconds." She walked toward the door, then turned to the couple one last time.

"Thank you for letting me inside." She closed the door behind her.

Elaine looked at Mark, mute with understanding. Gervais had gotten inside them in ways they'd never imagined.

St. John Mashrew

JennaTip #11: Clubbing

Sex clubs offer a variety of activities from watching to engaging in acts with others. Some clubs are permanent and others pop up now and again at either established dance clubs or bars or private homes or even entire hotels have been reserved for swinging parties and events.

While sex-club patrons pay a fee to enter the club, the club is not a brothel or a place of prostitution. The other participants are not paid for sex acts but also have paid to have access to the club facilities.

Sex clubs may have all open areas, be a series of different rooms, have themes, and be limited to heterosexual or homosexual couples only. As much variety as exists in the human imagination about sex, that much variety exists for sex clubs. Clubs may cater to particular fetishes, such as voyeurism, while others may be more of a free-for-all, once the entrance fee is paid, of course.

A good place to find a sex club or group to join is on the Internet. Do a lot of research, see if you can attend for a visitors' evening only, ask about safe-sex practices and requirements, and if you are in a long-term relationship, you better not be hiding this from your significant other because that's lying, and lying is not a basis for a good relationship.

Now here's a pretty little necklace any woman would gladly string about her neck.

Precious Gifts

"I'm going to grab us some dinner from Montevecchio," Damon announced as he emerged from his office and walked by the diamond case. Ansley smiled her agreement. She loved how handsome he looked in that charcoal raincoat of his, but Damon wasn't the type of man a woman complimented—he was well aware of his appeal to the opposite sex. She was just grateful that he was a decent boss and was kind to her. With others, he could be quite the . . . well . . . prick. Other employees said his smart-ass ways came naturally because of his ties to the famous Winston family. Damon alluded to being a relative of Harry Winston, but other than the name, there seemed to be little affiliation, as far as Ansley could see. But hers was not to question—hers was just to get a weekly paycheck.

Winston Jewelers stayed open late on Thursday nights and because of her need for extra money, she always worked that shift. With Christmas coming, she needed to work every available hour she could get. Eccentrics tended to shop on Thursday nights, she'd noticed, so when the door opened that night to admit a certain Mikhail Feher, she was not surprised in the least.

"Good evening, my pet," said the man as he approached the diamond case. He wore a black lacquered straw hat with a narrow brim, and a long black cape that stopped at his knees. To complete his ensemble, he wore a matching eye patch. A white Persian cat nestled in the crook of his arm and left a dusting of fur all over his black clothing. His skin bore slight pockmarks and his lips had a blue tint to them that made him look chilly. Ansley wanted to giggle, but had long ago learned how to stifle such impulses in reaction to Winston Jeweler customers.

"Happy holidays, sir," she said graciously. "How may I help you this evening?"

"Oh, in numerous ways, I should think," he said, leering at her with his one visible eye. She couldn't place his accent and suspected it was fake. Nevertheless, she did not lose her composure.

She stood before him, ignoring his untoward comment and waiting to hear exactly what his jewelry needs might entail. He eyed her up and down and she felt herself blush.

"What lovely pale skin you have, my dear. When I see such beauty, I think of rubies." He stared more intently at her. "Rooooo-beees." She smelled onions on his breath.

"Would you like me to show you some?" she offered.

"Yes, my sweet. But not just any old rubies. I would like you to show me a stunning necklace that you yourself would wear. A necklace that would accentuate that luscious porcelain neck."

She wished Damon would get back. This guy was beyond creepy.

Because the rubies were kept in a different case, she stepped away from him to walk to it. As she unlocked the case to withdraw the necklace she liked, the sound of his footsteps made her look back at him. She saw him close the shop's door, latch it, and flip the Open sign to Closed.

"What are you doing?" she asked, not moving from her spot.

"I am giving us some privacy. I don't like distractions when I shop for precious jewels."

"But I'm afraid you can't—"

He pulled a gun out from under his cape. "I can't do what, dear?"

She looked from the gun to his face and back again, then said nothing, even though her head pounded and her knees wanted to fold in half.

"Bring the rubies here, sweetness. What is your name, by the way?"

"Ansley," she said timidly as she fumbled with the keys in the case's lock. Eventually, she gained entry and extracted the most stunning ruby necklace she knew of.

"Ansley," he repeated. Her name sounded dirty on his lips. How soon would Damon get back? Surely, he'd know something was dreadfully wrong when he saw the door was locked and the CLOSED sign posted. But how long would it take him to send help? And just what did this weirdo intend to do with that gun? "Bend toward me so that I may put this necklace around your delicious throat."

He took the necklace from her hands; she bent forward across the counter trying to hide her trembling and he took much too long clasping it shut. While his inelegant fingers tried in vain to work the clasp mechanism, however, Ansley heard the sound of the back door. Damon had returned!

Still pointing the gun at her, Feher stared with icy concentration at her neck and the expensive rubies that adorned it. "Oh, Ansley, how you do justice to that superb necklace. I should like you to charge it to my account immediately."

As the man talked, Damon slipped into the sales floor area via the side door. He'd obviously gone in through the service entrance and taken the back hallway to get to this entrance. The door was behind the man with the gun so she was careful not to let her relief show on her face.

"Of course, sir. And what account is that?"

"Mikhail Feher, my dearest Ansley. You will have no trouble finding it. I am a frequent customer, although how I have never encountered your loveliness on my many visits, I cannot imagine."

As he spoke, Damon advanced. He, too, carried a gun—he must have retrieved it from the safe when he saw the CLOSED sign on the door. But rather than fire it, he used it to whack Mr. Feher across the side of his demented head. The blow was an unexpected one for the oddball customer and the man collapsed on the floor in response to it.

Approaching sirens blared and Damon moved to the front door to unlock it. Seconds later, police bounded in.

"Are you all right?" Damon asked Ansley. His intense blue eyes showed genuine concern, which made Ansley want to weep and embrace him. Instead, she nodded as she leaned against the counter for strength.

Feher came to just as the police handcuffed him. "Hey, man! You didn't say nothin' about cops!" There wasn't a trace of an accent, fake or otherwise. He shouted the words directly at Damon, who ignored him and watched coolly as the law dragged him out the door and put him in the backseat of the patrol car.

Ansley said nothing but understood what had just happened. Damon had set all of it up, which would explain the phony accent, the ridiculous costume, even the timing. Damon had wanted her to think he'd saved the day.

And damn it if she didn't find his efforts adorable. It meant he was interested in her!

She also understood that it would ruin everything if she pointed out the transparency of his plan. So, she continued to play the grateful damsel, formerly in distress.

"Oh, Damon. Thank goodness you came when you did. Did you see that he had a gun?"

"You poor thing. What a horrible incident. I should never have left you alone. Are you sure you're okay?" He took her hand from across the counter and held it tight.

"I'm better now. Really, Damon, I owe you my life. How can I ever repay you?"

His eyes met hers in meaningful, wordless intensity. "I have some ideas. Will you come downstairs with me?" His voice was quieter than she'd ever heard it.

Still holding her hand, he led her to the front door, which he locked, and then led her down the same stairs he'd used to come to her rescue. The office stockroom and the jewelry vault awaited them.

He dimmed the lights (Ansley never knew they could be dimmed), and pressed a button that filled the room with soft music (Joachim Brachan—his favorite—doing Christmas carols). "I have been waiting for this moment for a long time," he said, moving so close to her that she could feel his heat. The coziness of the vault seemed perfect for the intimate atmosphere he'd created. She just looked at him, waiting for him to kiss her, and in seconds, her lips met his.

He filled his palms with handfuls of her lustrous curls and gazed deeply into her eyes. "I would love to see you in the colors of the season," he whispered. "Something red."

He fingered her necklace, reminding her that she still wore it.

"And that's *all* I'd like to see you in," he added.

She let him undress her. Normally, the vault was bone-chillingly cold, but now she felt warm and protected. His hands touched her with feathery caresses, even as he unbuttoned buttons and unhooked her bra. At last, she stood before him wearing only the ruby necklace. He appraised her like he appraised the fine jewels he sold, spending several moments before he took her in his arms and kissed her so passionately she almost lost her balance.

"I'd love to do things on that jewelry table that would make Harry Winston shudder," he whispered in her ear. She giggled softly and went to the table, where she lay down on her back. Her breasts faced the ceiling. She spread her legs slightly and locked eyes with Damon.

He smiled—half devilish, half cherubic—and opened the drawer of his desk, which was filled with silver Christmas garland, left over from when they'd decorated the store. He proceeded to tie her ankles to the table legs but ran out of garland when he tried to restrain her wrists. With only four or five inches of the stuff left, his options dwindled. But then, he stripped off his pants to reveal a breathtaking hard-on, and grinning, he tied the garland around the base of it. Ansley laughed and he beamed.

He returned to the drawer and fished out a few random pieces of tinsel, and these he used to tickle her exposed body. As he caressed her nipples, they hardened to sharp points for him to lick. She ran her fingers through his thick, dark hair and he ran his through her furry triangle of pubic hair. No matter where he touched her, though, she seemed aware only of her pussy, throbbing and aching for him to kiss it. But she couldn't part her legs any wider because of the garland. Her frustration was sublime.

As he licked her nipple and stroked her furry little mound, she thought again about the pains he'd taken to frighten, then save her in order to impress her. Little did he know that she would have complied with his wishes even without all the theatrics. His fingers moved to her clit now, and she sighed as they found exactly the spot she needed them to touch.

"I want you to keep that necklace, Ansley," he said between licks at her breast. "It's my Christmas present to you."

"Thank you," she said, thinking about how the necklace was the least of his gifts.

Oni Nurani

I don't know about your experience with math and tutors, but this story has got to be pure fantasy.

Probabilities

He stopped dancing, not because he was tired, but because the sights on the beach that night demanded his full attention. The women were barely dressed and—bouncing and moving around to the wild music as they were—it was just better than 68 percent that one would lose her top. Yes, he was a math geek. Ever since his freshman year in high school, when he'd been tutored by a college girl who obviously never really saw him as a person from behind her geek-chic glasses even though he had jacked off to her image an entire semester. She was pretty in a general way, certainly not a stunner, but he was thirteen and she sat near him and he could smell the scent of her conditioner and it was like coconut. He was smelling a lot of coconut at the beach between the suntan oils and the piña coladas. That must be what got him thinking about Catherine? Caroline? He could not remember her name, just the coconut scent of her hair.

Dancing was fun. Bodies slamming against each other, everybody out for a good time, liquor flowing freely. Spring break was in full swing. His body thrummed to the rhythms of the dance band, which now played something vaguely '70s. As he was standing back, watching the show, a gorgeous blonde caught his attention and his breath stopped momentarily.

Though she was a couple of years older than many of the revelers on the beach, it worked to her advantage. The college girls' faces still had a little bit of baby fat to them, like they weren't yet formed into what they'd eventually be, while her face was striking and strong and gorgeous.

Perhaps he'd stared too long—why else would she have turned to meet his gaze and smile? He smiled back, never one to suffer from nervousness around women. Despite the crowds on the beach, the invisible thread that connected Aidan to the pretty blonde remained strong and constant. Finally, she laughed and made her way over to where he stood.

"Hi, I'm Cameron," she announced, when she got close enough to be heard.

"Hi. Aidan," he yelled, smiling, smiling, smiling.

"You should be dancing!" Her blue eyes sparkled and her complexion was flawless. She extended her hand confidently and clamped it on to his forearm. Before he knew it, he was following behind her, torn between watching her swaying backside and the other dancers.

When she'd pulled him out into the middle of a bunch of gyrating, unabashedly horny college students, she flashed a smile that made his head spin and immediately launched into a dance only a priest could resist. (And he wasn't too sure about them, either.) Her long, smooth torso slithered around him and he knew that if it weren't for the music, he'd hear her laughing like the vixen she most definitely was. It wasn't hard to surrender to her. In fact, it was natural.

She made no secret of watching his crotch, raising her eyebrows when his erection was obvious. He laughed, too, now proud of his response to her dancing. He knew every movement was for his benefit and he liked the attention. Since he'd started working out four years ago, he'd had his choice of women, but that only meant that quality became more important than quantity. And this luscious creature exuded quality of a type he had little experience with but a great desire to learn about.

His pulse raced, his hard-on pushed against his swim trunks, and as the moonlight cascaded across her sublime softness, he could imagine how her skin would feel under his roaming hands.

The music ended and a slow, soulful ballad replaced the primal beat. She tilted her head in a fetching mix of challenge and question. *Dare to dance with me again?* her expression asked.

Gently but firmly, he pulled her close to him and she complied gracefully. He could no longer see her face, but her warmth weakened his knees. Her silky hair tickled his cheek. She smelled like a blend of suntan oil and frozen drinks. Their bodies touched but only lightly—in the absence of the frenetic sounds and movement, quiet shyness overcame him. He could no longer hide behind outrageous antics and the distractions of others. Now she was close, moving to the music and in response to him.

"I feel like I know you," he said, thinking aloud. His words were uttered softly, a virtual whisper, intended only for her delicate ears.

She leaned into his hard-on. "I feel like I want to know you better," she replied.

The kisses he sprinkled on her neck elicited satisfying moans from her. He was encouraged and continued to touch his lips up along her neck to her earlobes, her temples, her cheek, and finally her mouth, which inexplicably tasted of coconut. As their tongues slid into each other's mouths, they held one another closer. Nobody else existed on Cancún, let alone the beach, as they kissed. His hands were in her hair, along her back, dangerously close to her perfect ass.

Without warning or apology, the music shifted back to a pulsating dance beat. Most couples separated without apparent regret, happy to get back to prancing and flirting. Cameron faced him and tossed her hair away from her face in one charming shake of her head.

"What would you say to a little break? I don't know about you, but I'd like to cool down a bit. Let's get a drink," she suggested.

He tried to hide his relief. The thought of dancing like a maniac again held no appeal for him—his woody was much too overwhelming. Slipping through the crowd toward the bar would buy him some time to return to normal, he hoped.

"Sure. Sounds good," he agreed.

But the walk did little to quell his excitement. By the time they reached the bar, he was as hard as he'd been during the slow dance. He hoped she wouldn't call attention to it, but he secretly hoped she'd notice it.

They walked to a quieter part of the beach, where the sounds of the party were less invasive. "This looks great," she decided, and sat on the sand confidently. He grinned and followed suit.

"So, Aidan," she began before taking a swig from her plastic cup. "Where are you from?" There was the slightest drawl to her inflection.

"Damn. You could tell I'm not a native."

She laughed. "Call it more probable than not . . ."

"I'm a student at UCLA. And you? No, lemme guess. Somewhere down south, right?"

"I was born in Alabama," she confessed. "Try as I might, the damn accent creeps up on me whenever I'm relaxed. I think I hide it from my students pretty well, though. They'd be merciless if I spoke the way my mama taught me!"

"You're a teacher?"

"I went to school in LA and then became a teacher right after. Guess we're neighbors," she said, smiling.

"I grew up in LA. Where do you teach?"

"Grayson High. I tutored there a lot once upon a time and got to know the school."

Aidan's head pounded with instant recognition. "Cameron Thomas. USC math tutor."

"Yes! How did you know that?"

They stared at each other as a parade of emotions marched across their faces. Her eyes lit up and she leaned back to appraise him. "Well, I'll be damned. Could you really be Aidan O'Connelly?"

He laughed, hoping his apprehension could be hidden underneath it. "That's me, all right. You look so different, Miss Thomas."

She laughed loudly—an outright hoot. "Miss Thomas?! Come on, Aidan. We've just been making out. I think you can call me Cameron."

Oh, God. Making out with his old math tutor, the object of a year's plus worth of fantasies. This couldn't be happening. He remembered Cameron as being sort of undefined and this woman was all definition and that definition was stunning. His confusion must have been obvious, because she explained what happened.

"Look at the girls around you here. I didn't know who I was or have real confidence. These girls drink to feel powerful. I realized a few years ago that I am powerful. That's the difference you're seeing. You certainly have filled out since last I saw you, but that's normal. Most boys change between ninth grade and eleventh grade. Your transformation, I must say, is very favorable." She paused as she assessed him like he was prey. "In fact, I'd say you're incredibly hot."

"Thank you," he mumbled, still trying to smile. He couldn't believe he was still hard, but his cock continued to strain his trunks. "So are you," he managed to say, mentally calculating that she was probably now about twenty-seven.

"Aidan, I do believe you're nervous," she observed. Her Alabama drawl reared its pretty head.

"A little, I guess. You have to admit, it's a bit weird."

She reached around behind her and untied her bikini top. When it fell from her exquisite tits, she grinned as he absorbed the vision. "You're not going to let ancient history get in the way of such an incredible connection, are you?"

Her pert, pink nipples extended almost as if to greet him. Her breasts were high and firm and so soft, so . . . His mouth surrounded a nipple before he had a chance to think any further.

He licked and sucked the tit of his old math tutor as she slipped a hand across his bulging crotch and stroked him through the fabric.

"I think it's time we took this party somewhere private," she said in a voice more breathy than she'd used earlier. She ran her fingers through his hair as he sucked her. "Let's go to my hotel room, Aidan."

Illuminated by only the moonlight, the room's furniture sat in shrouds of light. Their bodies did not separate from the moment Cameron closed the door behind them. Without meaning to, he pressed her against the door—hard—and kissed her deeply, now helping himself to handfuls of her glorious breasts, squeezing and kneading as his tongue explored hers. There was a feral quality to her movements that made the blood rush into his cock.

Somebody maneuvered the pair of them to the bed—it didn't matter who—but before he was horizontal, she'd adeptly removed his swim trunks. In the process, his erection had nearly walloped her in the face when it broke free of the garment. She giggled at the near injury and held his rock-hard cock firmly in her hand. She lay on the bed and pulled him down to her, using his cock like a leash.

He stripped her less smoothly, but efficiently, nonetheless. She hadn't put her bikini top back on before bringing him to the hotel. She sprinted into the lobby ahead of him, ignoring the shocked expressions of the guests checking in. She held the top up to her breasts, but it did little to cover what decency required. The elevator ride had been one long series of giggles and snorts as they realized what a show they'd just provided.

So, now, all that remained was to peel off her bottoms. She helped, which was sweet. Once she was naked, he could no longer control himself. Her pussy, scenting the room with a subtle hint of arousal and again that lingering sweetness of coconut, drew him with magical strength. His mouth followed the musky aroma and zeroed in on her juicy, swollen cunt lips. She spread her legs wide to show her approval. Amid her gasps and moans, he ate her, thoroughly and without hesitation. He ate her until she screamed with delight and his face was smeared with her cream.

Her convulsions had been so intense, he was surprised when she sat up and rolled on top of him. She sat on his dick and rode him wildly, slamming down on him relentlessly, bucking her way through another set of spasms as he let go with his own. Their shouts mingled and their tremors took on the same crackles of urgency. He'd never ejaculated so long and so hard, even when he masturbated. Her pussy squeezed every drop from his cock as if it knew just how much was there.

In spite of the grinding rhythms from the ongoing party on the beach, they eventually fell asleep, their bodies tangled in the aftermath of passion.

"What did you like best?" she asked, spooning up closer behind him, kissing his shoulder.

"I loved eating you," he confessed. And it was true that he could have done that all night and been happy.

"Mmm, I loved that, too. But I don't know if I liked my second orgasm better than my fourth." She laughed and he joined her. They'd made love so many times that night, neither of them could distinguish one come from another.

"Do you think the principal would object if I saw you once we're back in Los Angeles?" he asked, already hard and ready to slip into her wet heat once again.

"I was going to insist on it, actually. And I don't think I have to remind you what a math teacher is like when things don't add up the way she thinks they should."

"Something about probability factors, isn't that right?"

"Oh, you have so much to learn," she said, reaching around to grasp his morning thickness. "It's a good thing I'm here."

Justine Baum

Like the Energizer bunny, it looks like they'll just keep coming and coming and coming.

Getting the Party Started

They made their way through the house, through the softly lit parlor with abundant pillows and the big-screen television, sound muted. Most bodies were upright, but some were already horizontal and squirming—all were naked. He had a nice build, with well-groomed pubic hair a testament to his regard for genitalia. Pierced nipples, too. Very nice. She was much smaller, with a delicate snatch. Great succulent nipples. Her café au lait complexion suggested her ancestral roots were somewhere in South America. I'm a sucker for café au lait.

The man was the first to notice the steady stream of porn being played on the wide screen but the woman saw that the coffee table was strewn with glossy nudie magazines. Steps from the kitchen, where voices and laughter suggested friendly interaction, she had a small panic attack and clutched his arm.

I couldn't hear what they said, but I can only assume that the steady visual stream of tits, asses, cocks, pussies, moans, and slippery sloshing noises overwhelmed her. It scared the hell out of me the first time, too. And she was a tiny thing, which made her seem more vulnerable than she probably was. The way he soothed her, though, I could tell they had a good relationship—he hadn't forced her to come here. He seemed to appease her quickly enough and they continued toward the kitchen. They hadn't noticed me, so I stayed on my upholstered perch in the corner of the living room.

He was hard on arrival. I doubted they'd be in the kitchen very long—he looked like he was anxious to get down to business. So was I, but I'd learned patience. I knew what I was supposed to do, what was expected of me when I came here.

He held her hand and led her into the third room down the hall. Newbies usually began in a room, thinking it offered some protection from prying eyes. Ironic, since prying eyes are the reason most of them come to an orgy.

I waited a few minutes to give them time to get past the giggling stage. I thought about helping myself to a dildo from the welcome basket but decided to wait. I wanted my pussy to smell fresh when I approached Mr. and Mrs. First Time.

So, I spent the next fifteen minutes watching my friend Schuyler get fucked in every hole. It was hard not to cream while cocks pumped her voraciously, so I distracted myself with the porn on the big screen. Bored-looking women with sleazy guys—it helped keep me focused. Finally, I sauntered down the hall and just in the nick of time, too. They were in the middle of a charming little 69 when I leaned against the threshold to observe the fun.

They ate each other for a few minutes and then he stopped to reposition himself. He was ready to fuck his hot South American but then he caught sight of me. The pause prompted her to follow his gaze. *Voilà.* She saw me, too. I smiled as sweetly as I knew I could.

"Hi," he said with that jaunty tone so common among newcomers. The heady excitement had infused him with swaggering confidence.

"Hi," I replied. "I hope it's okay if I watch."

"It would be better if you joined us," she said.

I was flattered and did my best to blush. "Are you sure? I'm just as happy to watch." Yeah, right.

"Please come in. I'm Tripp, and this is Teresa."

"Colleen," I said as I approached the bed. "Would you mind if we got to know each other a bit before we start?" I asked the question for their benefit; I could have humped them both through the roof right then and there but wanted to let some tension build. Both of them eyed my big tits like they were dinner, so I thought it would be fun to delay gratification.

"Sure, sure," he said as Teresa sat up. They both scrambled off the bed and showed me to the sofa. As if I'd never been there before.

I sat down in front of the hefty black silicone dildo someone had so thoughtfully placed on the coffee table. A tiny vibrator lay on its side nearby. Perhaps Tripp and Teresa weren't the first people to use this room tonight. I was tempted to squat myself down on the dildo, but I'd long ago learned only to take toys from the welcome baskets stationed at every door—they were unquestionably clean.

Lots of porn mags covered the table. I glanced at them because a dark-skinned woman appeared on several of the pages. As I lingered over her plump ass, Tripp and Teresa flanked me on the couch.

I guess I'd waited longer than I wanted to join them because I found it too difficult to waste time on small talk. I sunk into the cushions, spread my legs, and grinned mischievously at my new friends. They grinned back.

While Tripp held out his thick meat for me, Teresa scooted over to the basket to withdraw a toy. If it was even half as impressive as the cock Tripp was jamming down my throat, I'd be one happy lady. His large tip stretched my mouth a bit, which I didn't find the least bit objectionable. He played with my tits while I sucked him.

Teresa's choice was a smooth, somewhat cool, vibrator that she turned on only when the thing had completely disappeared into my cunt. I sucked cock while she reamed me with the vibrator and licked my other nipple. To my surprise, she moved from my tit to my clit and frigged me with her tongue as if she had some experience. Maybe she did. Or maybe she was just emulating what Tripp usually did to her.

I juiced into her mouth like a papaya, lapsing into that state of mind I call "fuckhead." My brain took up residence in my pussy and all movement was determined by which hole would get serviced. I grabbed a handful of oversized balls and stroked Teresa's back. Pre-cum salted my tongue. My eyes roamed back to the voluptuous vixen in the porn mag and I imagined her sitting on my face as Teresa ate me and I sucked Tripp. The vibrator skimmed my G-spot and I was sure that I was staining the sofa with my profusely wet enjoyment.

Eyes (the prying kind) were on me but I shut mine to imagine a bigger crowd, a crowd that called out requests and waved rating cards like Olympic judges (they'd all be holding "10" cards, of course). I squeezed Tripp's tight sack just as my clit became the epicenter of my body, sending seismic waves through every artery, making me scream into the fleshy rod in my mouth.

Nobody was more surprised than I was. I usually had more control. Tripp and Teresa's enthusiasm was apparently more infectious than I thought.

In my semiconscious state, I let them carry me to the bed. Laughing they were undoubtedly as energized as I was by the voyeurs now crowding the doorway. I sensed one or two of them had slipped into the room, but I didn't much care—the more, the merrier. Oddly enough, I still didn't look to confirm my suspicions. The crowd in my imagination was more to my liking than the crowd at the door.

As Tripp and Teresa carried me, I had a sudden urge to remind them who was in control here, but instantly wondered why it mattered. I was still in fuckhead mode and liked the oblivion of it.

Once I was on my back, Tripp shoved a pillow under my ass and spread my legs. The scent of my well-worked pussy filled the room. Teresa lay down next to me and squished one of her luscious, compact tits against mine. Her body burned like a little furnace. She still held the vibrator she had pushed up my pussy and now slipped it into her own snatch as she leaned in to kiss me. She even tasted like café au lait—sweet and steamy.

She ran her exceptionally long fingernails along my spine while her tongue danced with mine. Our humid oral exchange made me dizzy—Teresa was an incredible kisser. I absently rubbed my clit, but it was her juices that were loud enough to be audible. She fucked herself with my cream-covered vibrator and French-kissed me into a heightened state of abandon.

When Tripp's mushroom head pushed past my slit, I yelped and my eyes suddenly shot open. I saw the faceless crowd, saw Teresa's manicured hand fucking herself wildly, watched as Tripp's beautiful cock plunged into me and then reemerged, over and over, each time coated with more of my glistening juice. I rubbed my clit and let the second wave of tremors crash through me. I lost track of the crowd when my eyes rolled up inside my forehead.

A few gasps punctuated a lovely, reverent silence as I spiraled downward from my come. A familiar voice floated through the quiet.

"Colleen, you little slut. You've done it again."

I opened my eyes languidly, trying to control my glee. Tripp and Teresa faced Schuyler abruptly, with the kind of fear in their eyes she surely appreciated. No matter how many times we played this game, it never failed to get her off.

"I've been watching you. Fucking my girlfriend like she was

yours. Well, look what you've done now," she purred. I looked at her even though I knew she'd be whipping her pussy to the consistency of butter as she walked toward us. Schuyler was one of the few people I knew who could masturbate and walk at the same time.

Tripp and Teresa were in for a memorable night. I just hoped I could keep up with all of them.

Olivia Ulster-Reed

This is a real booty-and-the-beast sort of tale. Who wins at the end? The loser, perhaps?

Power Play

The woman looked familiar, but I was too high to think about her very long. When I caught Kyle checking her out, though, I paid more attention.

I hated it when these kinds of bitches came to the rave. They could have anybody they wanted and they could find them at all the beautiful-people-only parties they got invited to—why did they feel the need to come here and hang out with the same people they'd probably cross the street to avoid at any other time?

Kyle loved booty and this bitch had it for days. Even with all that long, light brown wavy hair like a fucking princess and a halter that had less fabric than a jockstrap, the woman's ass commanded attention. Maybe it was the way she swung it when she walked or the way her jeans clung to her like a horny lover. She had a body that I felt certain made her money somehow—it was too perfectly rounded and firm. She looked way too confident to be a prostitute. There wasn't a shred of fear or the desire to please in her demeanor. I guessed she was some kind of model.

I followed Kyle as he slowly made his way toward the piece of ass that promised more trouble by the minute. Kyle knew I was on his heels but he wouldn't care, because that's where I often was, until he wanted to play with me. Then I was front and center—or wherever he wanted me to be.

Heads turned as Kyle passed through the dancing, screaming, posing, and tripping crowd, but I was used to that. Even liked it. Who wouldn't stare at a six-foot-two-inch bald, black man with an earful of piercings and a snake tattoo that wound around his neck? He wore nothing but black, mostly leather, and everything about him announced his profound distaste for being fucked with.

If he'd asked me, I could have told him that this self-centered little cunt was slumming tonight and that she got her rocks off by conquering men and then disappearing. But maybe Kyle knew that already. Sometimes he knew a lot more than I gave him credit for, especially when it came to head games.

As we approached Miss Goddamn America, I noted the flawless complexion, the almond-shaped eyes, and the firm, full tits barely covered by her halter. She wore a stunning swirl of burnished silver at her neck that only added to her singularly powerful aura.

I didn't hear everything Kyle said to the woman. Fragments came to me, though, that I pieced together. "Got it goin' on," came from Kyle in that dizzying baritone he knew how to use so well. "Just checking things out" and "can't stay long" from her, without a fluttering eyelash or girlish smile. The woman's pupils were enormous, but her speech was controlled and calm. Hard to tell whether she was fucked up or not.

Kyle nodded toward the beat-up metal door near the far west corner of the space. I knew what was in there because Kyle and I had screwed each other and others (not always separately) in that decrepit little room with the pseudo-Persian rugs, random and useless office equipment and furniture, and cheap incense. It was supposed to be an exotic getaway from the pulsating madness in the main room, but really it was just an upholstered pen decorated by some deluded hippie who thought it made a groovy make-out room. It was also great for drug deals that were a little more complicated than usual.

So, Kyle led the beauty-queen bitch to the room, but her walk left no question that it was her decision to join him, that no coercion whatsoever had occurred. I figured she had a jones for some dark meat and as soon as she rode Kyle's monster bone, she'd be off on her next hunting expedition. She disgusted me and I was a little disappointed in Kyle for playing into her plans.

Once we were all in the grungy little room, I slammed the door behind us. The Duchess of Attitude shot me the same kind of glance I'd bet she also gave her maid when she missed a pubic hair in the bathtub.

"Who's this?" she asked Kyle, hands on hips, head tilted in my direction. There was no outrage in her voice, though. She stood there like an executive collecting information.

"This is Poe. She goes where I go."

"Does she have sex with the same people you do?"

"Yeah."

She looked at me finally, quickly summarizing me as only privileged little bitches know how. "I'm Kasey," she said flatly. "I guess we'll be fucking."

I surmised that we were the same age, roughly twenty-four. She was several inches taller than I, a good five feet ten with those high-heeled boots. I knew why Kyle was hot for her—I was getting wetter myself every second I was near her.

She whipped off her halter. "Kyle thinks he can break me sexually," she smiled as she spoke to me but I had trouble not staring at her gorgeous tits. I'd seen—and sucked—lots of silicone in my time with Kyle, and I wasn't at all sure these mounds were fake. I hated her even more and refused to respond to any of her remarks.

"I know I can," Kyle chuckled as he opened one of the drawers of the abused and antiquated desk. He withdrew the restraints he'd used on me many times before. "I'm going to control you with these."

"Yeah, right. A pussy as powerful as mine laughs at your weak, pathetic ropes. We should make a wager—I stand to make a lot of money on this game."

I would have expected Kyle to unzip his fly and unleash the biggest dick this supermodel had ever seen. I swear I saw the thought flicker over his face, but he didn't act on it. Instead, he told Kasey to take her pants off.

"You want 'em off, you take 'em off," she replied. From the perfection of her breasts to the allure of her sexual core with her sculpted ass, trim but rounded thighs, flat but feminine tummy, her power emanated through her skin-tight jeans. Under that fabric breathed a force I knew Kyle wanted to confront, battle, and conquer.

But I also knew he couldn't. Not alone. He needed my help.

The bitch was winning the power struggle. Kyle obeyed her, inching her zipper down. The scent of her crotch transfixed him.

The two of us—Kyle and I—had fucked so many people together. If they weren't cowed by his physique or his big, black skinhead, they became whimpering little fools when he pulled out his fleshy ten-inch punisher. We were accustomed to being in control, to wielding the power, to commanding the action. Never did we wait with bated breath for a sweet booty or juicy twat—they waited for us. We never imagined anything different.

But Kasey was different. When we stripped off her jeans and thong and she stood before us naked and strong, our awed silence spoke volumes. We weren't muted by her beauty, formidable though it was. We were hushed into reverence for her that both fascinated and infuriated me.

"Is that where I should lie down?" she asked, pointing at the lumpy, afghan-draped, foam mattress in the corner.

"Yes, that's right. Put that fine booty down, bitch. You'll wanna be comfortable when you lose it."

"Fuck you," she laughed and took her time finding just the right spot for each of her limbs on the unwelcoming mat.

"Tie her wrists, Poe. I'll get her ankles."

I hesitated. I knew what had to be done here and wanted to make sure Kyle did it. He didn't like it when I challenged him while he was working pussy. So, I tied Kasey's wrists but watched him in my peripheral vision. To my surprise, he caught my eye, as if to ask for my assistance as he started to restrain her ankles.

"Wider," I said quietly. It was vital to keep her as splayed as possible. She may have known the power of her crotch, but I knew that the wider she was spread, the more exposed and vulnerable she would be.

A flash of gratitude lit his eyes—only someone who knew him would have seen it. A second later, he was back to his usual self-containment.

Kasey willed his gaze with her own, directing his attention to her elegant, neatly trimmed pinkness. Her slopes and valleys were not that different from any other woman's, but both Kyle and I hesitated to touch her. Like we'd defile her or something. The power of her moist center held us captive until I came to my senses and launched into action.

"I'm ready when you are, Kyle." I peeled out of my own black jeans, jarring him out of his trance.

"Yeah. I'm gonna play with her until she screams." He touched his fingers to her glistening labia.

"I don't scream, homeboy," Kasey pointed out.

"Is that so?" He stood now and unzipped his jeans, slowly unfurling his meat for full effect. She didn't gasp or giggle, but a crooked grin danced on her stunning face.

"Not bad. I like a duel that's evenly matched."

It was a breathtaking tool and she fucking knew it. Even in

her world of surgically enhanced bodies, she couldn't possibly have seen a cock more stupendous than this one. She could lie there acting all cool but there was no way she wasn't hungry for Kyle's dick. Every time I saw it, I wanted to stick it into some hole of mine. No woman could be unaffected by the pure size and heft of it.

So I sucked him while he fingered her to show her how good it was. Show her what she was missing. It pissed me off that Kyle was harder than I'd ever seen him. Fucking a skinny white beauty must have been a bigger turn-on for him than I thought.

I let my spit dribble down his shaft and nearly gagged myself on his thickness. I ate him like he was my life force. I grabbed his ass and shoved his cock as far down my throat as I could.

"Yeah, baby. Eat your daddy." His deep voice resonated like a drum in the ugly little room.

He teased her with his fingers and every now and then when I glanced over, I saw her clit get bigger and pinker. Her scent was the only aroma in the room—it was like I didn't have a pussy of my own. Before I had time to censor myself, I too had one hand between her legs, finger-fucking her defenseless slit, waiting for moans that eventually came.

After a little while, Kyle gently removed me from his cock so he could position himself like a ravenous dog between Kasey's legs. With big, wide strokes from his melon pink tongue, he lapped at her pussy, as hungry for her as I was for him. I no longer felt jealous as much as I felt like a fan rooting for her team. I didn't know what a win or a loss would look like, but I was dead set on staying to the end of the game.

And that's when I saw it—the veins in her neck, the parted lips, and the pleading eyes. Her control wavered before our eyes and I couldn't remember being any more aroused than I was at that exact moment.

Kyle saw it, too, and instantly moved in for the kill. He aimed his cock at the bulls-eye of the juiciest, most powerful cunt ever to cross his path, then slammed it deep inside her, over and over, until her cries testified to her surrender.

As tears rolled out of the corners of her eyes, I whipped my pussy to a speedy climax. Unable to contain myself while Kyle emptied his balls into this conquered queen, I gripped his steely arm as I came in erratic surges and spasms, thrilled that he'd won. Thrilled that we'd won.

But as she lay there, quietly regaining her composure, I wondered whether, instead of showing her where the power was, we'd actually given her the gift of pleasure. Damn the bitch—everywhere she went, she got the best, 'cause that's what Kyle is, the fucking best.

Neil Truitt

This story doesn't let you see it coming, though there's plenty of coming going on.

The Dante Effect

With skin oiled to simulate a sheen of sweat, the stripper hit the stage. Not a hormone in the audience was undisturbed—every one of the thirteen women gasped, gaped, or howled as the man wiggled about in a white sailor's uniform that strained at the seams.

Janice leaned over to me and had to shout over the sultry horns of "Night Train" from the club's speakers. "Oh my God, Danielle! Isn't this the guy who fucked Michelle at her bachelorette party?"

I nodded and smiled mischievously. "Yup."

"What's his name again?"

"Dante!"

I was shocked that anybody would forget the name of a body so hard and finely sculpted, but not surprised at all that what he did with it instantly reignited Janice's memory. Nobody would ever forget the image of Michelle bent over and squealing as Dante gave her what her endless flirtations had earned her. He'd come highly recommended by some friends and after Michelle's bachelorette party, I understood why. Dante was the kind of send-off into matrimony that every girl needed.

Especially Lauren.

I looked over at her to gauge her reaction to the magnificent Dante. She was giggling and blushing. I wouldn't have expected anything else. Despite Lauren's hot body and pretty face, she is incredibly shy. I suppose that's what Lee finds so appealing about her. He always did feel safer with women who didn't threaten him much.

But I can't resist a good piece of drama, so I had called him yesterday to tell him about the party.

"Hey, Lee, how are you?"

"Oh, hi, Danielle. Lauren's not here right now."

"Oh, I didn't call to talk to her. I wanted to talk to you."

His voice got that smidgeon of panic that I recognized so well. "You did?"

"Yeah, I wanted to tell you that I think Lauren would love it if you surprised her at the party tomorrow."

"But it's just for women, isn't it? I wouldn't want to intrude on all that girl stuff." He laughed nervously.

"Don't be silly! I really think she'd like it. Promise you'll drop in?"

"Well, okay. If you think it's a good idea."

And now, just as Dante grabbed his crotch, yanked the fabric, and separated the front of his sailor pants from the back, I noticed Lee lurking in the shadows near the kitchen. Every time the swinging doors would open or close, he was backlit by the kitchen's bright light. He didn't venture forward, toward the action. He merely stared at it, like a zoologist might observe the copulation of rare birds.

Dante had tossed all his articles of clothing to various audience members and now gyrated on stage wearing only a G-string bulging with promise and a white, wicked smile. He rubbed his cock through the flimsy, overworked fabric as he sent Lauren the most penetrating stare she'd probably ever received. A couple of the girls shouted obscenities and invitations—Jill even threw her panties at him—but he didn't waver. His goal was Lauren and everybody was slowly beginning to understand that. Including Lee, I noticed when I glanced back at him.

Dante left the stage and circulated among the clamoring females. They copped as many feels as they could, caressed whatever was presented to them, and even stuffed money and business cards into whatever part of the G-string was accessible. His butt was hard enough to bounce quarters off and his abs rippled with strength. When he danced near me, I became all too aware of how wet he'd already made me and how much I wanted to see the slab of meat that threatened to explode from his tiny briefs any second. His eyes made intermittent contact with each of us at one point or another, but his true attentions were clearly on Lauren, just as I'd specified when I hired him.

He straddled her, flanking her lap with his brick-house thighs. The hoots and hollers were constant now, and Lauren's face was a deep pink as she did her best to avoid looking at Dante's basket. He shimmied his hips closer to her face until she finally had to confront it in all its throbbing masculine glory. He was so close she was probably breathing in the scent of his balls, could probably see the tiny dot of pre-cum soaking through his G-string. When she finally stopped giggling, he thrust his hips toward her face as if to fuck her mouth.

Dante had definitely pushed her past the blushing debutante phase and when the kitchen door opened, I saw that Lee realized it, too. What was Lee thinking, I wondered? Had he ever seen Lauren so enthralled by the prospect of a man's power before? Had he ever elicited that kind of hunger? He remained rooted to the spot at the back of the room, pondering and worrying.

Dante looked down at her now with a gleam in his eye. Sarah reached into the narrow space between Dante's crotch and Lauren's face and pulled the nearly useless material down. Out popped the legendary flesh snake that got him this gig in the first place.

It practically rolled itself out of the tight, airless space it had been forced into while he danced. Sarah, the perpetrator, jumped back in justifiable fear at the sight of it. I wanted to burst with delight at the awe Dante's cock inspired and when I got a glimpse of the terror on Lee's face, it was all I could do not to cackle.

"Your friends are pretty audacious," Dante said to Lauren, smirking. His knob hovered about an inch from her chin and rendered her speechless.

And why not? Dante's ten-inch cock, thick with readiness, was not only smooth and just the right shade of burgundy, but it had that friendly, come-hither quality that women adored. Some cocks just knew how to draw women, and Dante's was one.

He knew how to seize the moment. He wiggled his hips to caress Lauren's cheek with his beautiful meat. "Oooohs" and "aaaaahs" dotted the audience. When Lauren closed her eyes to enjoy the full and undoubtedly profound effect of this movement, it was time for *me* to seize the moment.

"Hey, check it out," I said. "Isn't that Lee back there?"

They descended on him like vultures. Meanwhile, Dante led the starry-eyed Lauren to the stage. I stayed seated, where I could see everything.

Lauren didn't flinch as Dante kissed her mouth and slowly ran his hands over her sexy ass and through her long, dark hair. Was she aware that Lee was present? Dante took handfuls of her big tits and squeezed. Lauren bit her lip and closed her eyes.

The ladies had pushed Lee to the foot of the stage, where Dante and Lauren both worked toward stripping Lauren. "Aren't you going to say hello to your fiancée, Lee?" Jill taunted.

Lauren's fantastic tits were free now and Dante had a big juicy nipple in his mouth. At the sound of Lee's name, Lauren did turn to the group, but upon seeing Lee, her reaction was not one of shame or guilt or even concern. She stared at him with half-lidded eyes as Dante suckled her tits and filled his palms with her luscious ass cheeks. She was naked except for her high heels.

"Jesus! He's hard! Look at this!" Sarah announced, pointing to Lee's prominent bulge. When the other women shifted their attention from the performers to Lee's crotch, Sarah decided to unzip him and help herself to his confused erection. She pulled it out of his pants and the women howled.

He cut a sad and pathetic figure, standing there with his painfully average cock and middle-class sexual sensibilities. Although he had no idea how to stop Dante from giving pleasure to Lauren, neither had he any clue about how to hide his excitement.

Dante didn't pause. He bent Lauren over just as he had manipulated Michelle months before. Lauren's solid, heavy tits pointed toward the floor and her ass tilted skyward, waiting to be reamed by Dante's formidable ramrod. Lauren's pink folds glistened under the hot lights. In her high heels and immodest position, she looked every inch the wanton exotic dancer and Lee's expression went from excited to transfixed in seconds. Dante inserted himself slowly into Lauren, making her hungrier for him the longer he made her wait. He spread her open wide with his hands to let us all see what he was taking. Lauren kept trying to slam herself against him but his strong hands kept her still so he could fuck her as he wanted—at his pace, in his time.

Myself, I wanted to bend Lee over and fuck him as hard as Dante was now fucking Lauren. I wanted to fuck him and every man who had made the same stupid, uninformed choice for a lifetime partner. He had stopped dating me to be with someone less threatening, less sexually demanding. He thought Lauren was going to be it, but after tonight, he'd understand how wrong he was. All he would have to do was look at her now, with her cunt full of Dante's fat, pumping cock, and he'd have to realize that he could never satisfy her. Maybe he'd never be able to fully satisfy any woman.

Oh, the sweet dichotomy of fear and lust on poor Lee's face

as Sarah jerked him off and Dante screwed Lauren! Adrenaline made it impossible for me to sit still any longer. I walked up to the stage and handed a microphone to Lauren.

"Tell Lee how it feels," I instructed.

She was so dazed, I don't think she knew what I was talking about for the first few seconds that she held the microphone. Then, as the final centimeters of Dante's cock disappeared inside her and started to thrust, she took on new life.

"*Oh yes!*" she yelled. "Why can't you fuck me this hard, Lee? Do you see what he's doing to me?" Dante rammed her harder and faster, causing her to drop the microphone. I picked it up and handed it to her again. "Big fucking cock!" she sputtered.

When she moaned her come into the sophisticated sound system, Lee let loose with his own strain of happiness, spraying several of the women who restrained him, then instantly going soft. Dante then pulled out of Lauren and released a geyser of spunk that sounded like a splat of mashed potatoes when it landed. He caught some of it in his hand and massaged it into Lauren's ass cheeks as he smiled at the awestruck group.

I don't know what happened after that because I left. I'm half-expecting that tomorrow's wedding won't go off as planned, though.

Leigh Malone

*You can't have kids without sex and then you don't have
sex because you have kids.*

Summer Camp
in February

His skin tingled. His heart raced. A persistent smile curled the
outer corners of his lips.

It was Friday afternoon, which meant he was on his way to see
Linnea. And that was more than enough to get his motor racing.

He loved teaching and he loved his students, but no day
brought him more joyful anticipation than the one that came at
the end of the workweek, the one that allowed him to put the
job aside and concentrate on her. Even though Linnea had kids
of her own—kids that often kept him from enjoying her to the
extent he might have liked—seeing her along with them was still
a thousand times better than not seeing her at all.

Her car was reassuringly parked in the driveway when he arrived. For once, no children were coming or going. In fact,
none of them came out to meet him, which disappointed him a
little. Even Sparky bounded out of the van, expecting to frolic
with somebody small but dancing around pointlessly upon dis-
covering nobody was there.

But then Linnea emerged, looking freshly showered and re-
freshed. It was unusual for her to be able to leave work early on
a Friday, which she would have had to do to look so right out of
the shower by 5:00. He smiled at the vision of her as she approached.

"Hey, gorgeous!" Greg called out. "You're home early today."

Her beautiful lips touched his and lingered a moment. He inhaled, as he always did whenever she kissed him. He never liked to miss any opportunity to savor her scent. She usually smelled like the girly hair products she spent her day around but tonight he caught more of her natural sweetness, a deep but lighthearted aroma of bar soap and cinnamon. Or was it vanilla? Her body heat tickled his nostrils.

"Yes, I am home early today. Just needed a little time off, you know?"

He followed her into the house, watching her body move in the little pink skirt she wore. Her strong, shapely legs moved with confidence, and that ass . . . Just seeing it made his mouth water. Just as he was about to comment on how hot she looked, something else distracted him.

All over the living room, candles in various shapes and sizes burned and shades were drawn. The room became instant midnight, sparkling with promise. Some of the candles were scented, filling the room with a mix of pine and rain, like a forest in a storm. Soft music with a South American rhythm floated from the stereo. A bottle of champagne sat at a jaunty angle in the silver ice bucket.

He looked at her and saw that she was beaming. "Where are the children?" he asked cautiously.

"Summer camp," she grinned, closing the front door.

"In February?"

"It's summer *somewhere* in the world," she shrugged and winked.

"Seriously, sweetheart. Are they not here?"

"Seriously. They're gone for the weekend. We have th~
to ourselves."

If his mind had been a jumble of hopes and im~
minutes earlier, now it reeled with unrestraine~
with Linnea! For the entire weekend!

"Champagne?" she asked, eyes gleaming. She took the bottle from its bed of ice and positioned it to pop the cork.

"Yes, please," he said, his grin so wide he felt like The Joker.

She poured two glasses of the bubbling concoction, handed him one, and raised hers in a toast. "To grown-up fun."

He laughed. "To grown-up fun." Their glasses clinked.

She put her glass on the coffee table. Keeping her eyes on him, she peeled off her white top, revealing a pretty white bra that barely contained her breasts.

"All this fire making you warm?" he asked, one eyebrow raised.

She said nothing but didn't lose her mischievous grin. With one expert movement, she unhooked the back of her bra and tossed it behind her. "There," she said. "That's better."

It was true what they say about candlelight—it illuminated her beautifully. She was fired with an unearthly glow that seemed to come as much from within her as from the dozens of tiny flames around the room. Her hair framed her face like it might in a Dutch master's painting. She stood before him, topless, looking simultaneously soft and strong.

Her nipples pointed at him, as if they'd been waiting all day to see him and now that he was there, they demanded his attention. He was happy to oblige them, yet he couldn't stop looking at her, noticing how smooth her skin looked and how little tension her body carried.

"I thought these might make perfect hors d'oeuvres," she purred, straddling his chair and positioning her luscious breasts just inches from his mouth. "I've had the recipe for ages," she giggled.

Her nearness sent waves of warmth toward his face and chest. She removed his shirt the way he'd taught her and suddenly the warmth morphed into a million tiny flashes of electric current, weakening and melting his defenses. What defenses? He'd lost those when he met Linnea so many months ago.

She held one breast in her hand and slowly brought it to his mouth. He flicked it with his tongue, an instinct that was also born from a desire to see if it might get harder or bigger than it already was. He blew on the film of saliva he left behind, making her moan. He couldn't give the nipple any more time to swell—he needed it in his mouth. Now.

She pushed her breast farther into his mouth. He sucked in not only her nipple and areole but also an entire mouthful of tit-flesh, intent on consuming whatever would fit between his cheeks. His tongue bathed her breast in hot moisture as she fed it to him.

When his mouth was completely and utterly full, she let go of her breast and moved her hands to his chest. In long, sweeping motions, she ran her nails along his pecs and across his wide chest. Back and forth, up and down, her nails roamed the landscape of his muscles, breastbone, and shoulders, all the while avoiding his nipples. He knew she'd save those for last. She'd wait until he wanted to burst, until his heart pounded so violently that he thought he'd go into cardiac arrest. She'd do that because that's what he loved best.

He sucked. She scratched. He could smell her more strongly than ever now. Was it her pussy, kicking into overdrive? He groaned into her tit, a sign that he needed his nipples stimulated.

She understood, as she always did. Between thumb and forefinger, his nipples became her captives. She squeezed, twisted, tweaked and he winced, swallowed, squeaked.

Pleasure emanated from his chest and slithered up to brain, making him dizzy. He didn't stop sucking, no what her fingers decided to do with his nipples.

"And now it's time for the main course," s' hoarseness in her voice. "It will be served in

Reluctantly, he released his oral clamp on her tit to allow her to get off his lap. He followed her into the kitchen, confused but intrigued.

She lay down on the kitchen counter, hiking up her skirt high enough to reveal that she wore no panties. She wiggled herself to a spot where the edge of the counter aligned with the point where her thighs met her ass. Then she spread her legs wide to give him a good look at her slick, pink folds, glistening just for him.

"Serve yourself, partner. This is buffet style." She had propped herself up on her elbows so she could see him between her legs.

He wheeled forward, stopping when his wheels met the counter. She then slid closer to him, draping her legs over his shoulders. All he'd have to do was lean forward slightly and he'd be in an aromatic vortex of pussy.

Naturally, he leaned forward.

Her wet heat accosted him. Her pussy scent, intense and earthy, drew him toward her dripping cunt. He barely had time to even look at what she offered—and he did want to look because visuals were important. He liked to file them away in his mind to refer to later in his fantasies. But there was no opportunity for that kind of memorization now. Her sweet pussy cream begged for his tongue. With one long, wide lap of his tongue, he tasted her.

And that one taste triggered an endless series of licks and swirls, some at her swollen clit, others along the puffy slopes of her labia. She tasted slightly different at her clit than she did near her hole, he noticed. Slightly saltier. He loved these variations, and the more he sampled her, the more tiny differences he noted.

He saved her slit for last. He licked up what wetness he could ore sliding his tongue inside, darting in and out of her for a little while and then trying to stay inside while wagging his tongue. She seemed to love whatever he did, and he was content to do it for as long as she could stand it.

He smiled inwardly as he wondered if they'd ever find time to get to the champagne that weekend.

Heather Willis

Dungeons and Damsels

The redhead lay on her back with her big, round breasts sticking up in the air. Her legs were spread so that when the blonde finished licking her luscious pink nipples, she could make her way down to that steamy place between her legs. The redhead saw him standing at the window, watching, but didn't say anything. Instead, she ran her tongue along her lips before she wagged it provocatively at him. The look in her eyes said "Don't you wish it was you licking my body?" He wanted it to say, "I wish it was you licking my body." But that's not what they said, of that he was sure. She was clearly very happy with the blond woman's attentions.

The blonde was enjoying herself so much she didn't seem aware he was standing just outside peering in, watching as she ran her tongue all over the redhead's breasts. The redhead was moving her hips all around, begging for cock, or so he imagined.

Finally, the blonde hovered over the redhead's furry little muff, nuzzling it before she dove in for the sweet wetness. The redhead smiled at him now and even seemed to laugh, though he couldn't hear anything through the window. When the blonde buried her face between the redhead's legs, he had to remind himself to breathe. She really went to town on her willing friend, shoving her tongue up her cunt, rubbing her nose against her clit, and was not even interested in coming up for air.

The redhead's hips were gyrating wildly now. She ground her

pussy into the blonde's face, forcing her to eat more, faster. Both women had such perfect bodies—long legs, long hair, smooth, flawless skin. He imagined how soft and supple they must feel. The thought made him rock-hard.

But when the blonde paused to reach behind her, to a spot he couldn't see, and retrieve a strap-on dildo, he stopped thinking and started just doing. He whipped out his throbbing member and started stroking. With his palm full of his own needy rod, he stared as the blonde slipped on the complex apparatus. He marveled at the way she never stopped leering at the redhead, as if she were about to conduct strange experiments on the pretty crimson-tressed creature.

With the big black dildo hanging from her pubis, the blonde held it in her hand, much like he held his own monster hard-on. She pointed it at the spread-eagled redhead in a threatening, menacing kind of way, clearly letting her know what to expect next. Sure enough, she stuffed the rubbery cock deep into the firecrotch. The blonde rammed her so suddenly and so hard she forced her to cry aloud.

The blonde liked the reaction she got, so she reamed her harder.

In his mind, he became that silicone dildo, pumping that beautiful, wet pussy, feeling those juices spread all over his balls. Stroking his dick in sync with the blonde's thrusts into the redhead, he beat his meat without inhibition and made eyes at the redhead, who made eyes right back.

Unfortunately, the blonde noticed and did not find the exchange between him and the redhead to her liking. She stopped fucking the juicy strawberry, though she kept the dildo in the dripping ginger snatch. She assessed him with a critical, unforgiving eye, particularly when her gaze lingered on the growing out of his fist.

He froze, waiting to see what would happen nex

call the cops? Scream? Ask him to join in? She stalked toward him. From the fury in her eyes, he doubted he was going to be invited to enjoy himself, but it didn't look as though she would be calling the cops, at least.

She walked around to the door and flung it wide.

Her nipples, hard and angry, stuck out like mini-rifles, ready to shoot. They were flushed a deep shade of pink. Her eyes, large, green and fiery, flashed like ice shards.

"What the fuck do you think you're doing?"

"I was watching," he stammered.

"Pervert," she spat. "You know what we do with perverts around here?"

"No."

"We punish them. Get in here, you sick bastard. You've got punishment coming."

He stepped through the doorway when she stepped away from it. Once inside, he saw that there was nothing in the room except for the bearskin rug where the redhead still lay. The room's walls were painted black, which created the illusion of no walls at all. Mirrors completed the stark effect.

As she sauntered into the room ahead of him, he noticed for the first time that she wore stiletto heels. The shoes put a sway into her walk that made him salivate.

"Get up, Andrea," she said to the redhead. "We've got punishment to administer."

Andrea, too, wore stiletto heels and when she got to her feet, he noted she was even taller than the blonde. Legs that went up to her neck . . .

"What's your name, jerk?" The blonde addressed him.

"Victor."

"Victor," she said as if it were a bug she found in her soup.

"You will do whatever we tell you until I am satisfied you've been punished enough. If I tell you to stick your cock into someone or something, you'll do it. If I tell you to bend over and eat pussy until you choke on it, you'll do that. If we tell you to mop the floor, you'll even do that. Do you understand, *Victor?*" The emphasis she put on his name was designed to make him feel small. It worked.

"Yes, I understand."

Her hands flew to her hips. "You will address me as Mistress. Can you handle that, Victor?"

"Yes, Mistress."

"Do you like to eat assholes, Victor?"

"Depends on the owner of the asshole, Mistress."

She turned to Andrea. "Isn't this amusing? We've got a budding comedian here tonight." She faced him again. "You don't get to choose the asshole, you twit. You will eat whatever ass is put before you and you'll like it. We will begin with mine."

She turned around, bent at the hips, and exposed her hairless bunghole to him. "Eat my ass!" she barked.

He knelt behind her, grasped her firm, muscled thighs, and prepared to taste her sphincter.

"Did I say you could touch me?"

"You said I should eat you, Mistress," he countered.

She sighed with supreme exasperation. "Only your tongue can touch me, moron. Eat my ass without touching me."

He stuck out his tongue carefully and approached the perfectly pink asshole.

The blonde's asshole smelled like pussy—sweet, dripping pussy. He circled her tight hole with his tongue, as instructed, feeling every tiny fold, every little wrinkle that comprised her beautiful poop chute. Every inch of her crack was hairless, so nothing could hide from him. She hadn't actually forbid him to enjoy it.

And she liked it, too, because the longer he lingered between her cheeks, the wetter she got. When her hips began making circular motions into his face, he groaned. If his mouth weren't full of her ass, he would've told her how good she tasted.

"Are you making noises back there?" she snapped over her shoulder.

Reluctantly, he pulled away from her fleshy cheeks. "Yes, Mistress."

"Well, I don't like it. Fuck Andrea's breasts while I think about what to do with you next."

She and her luscious ass stepped away from his drooling mouth. He knew better than to complain. The scent of her cunt had seeped into his pores and he continued to smell her even after she walked away. After a few deep breaths, he shifted his attention to Andrea, who now approached him with a gleam in her eye that would've frightened lesser men.

Her breasts bounced with every step she took toward him. He grinned at her, which the blonde didn't like.

"Did I say you could flirt with her? Just fuck her breasts, you shithead."

Andrea's back was to the Mistress, so the blonde didn't see the redhead wag her tongue at him as if she were flicking the tip of his cock. He forced himself not to react, not to say, "Suck my cock, you slut." She reached up, squeezed her healthy, round boobs together, and pushed them toward him.

"You're supposed to fuck these," she purred, keeping them just inches from his face.

"That'll be pretty hard if you stay up there," he pointed out.

The blonde appeared next to him and slammed a wooden

chair down hard on the floor by his feet. "You're too stupid to know this, but only a whore gets on her knees, especially to let scum like you fuck her breasts. Did you grow up on a farm or something, Victor?" She sneered.

"No," he mumbled.

"No, *what?*"

"No, Mistress."

"Stand on the chair, Victor. Fuck Andrea's breasts that way."

The chair looked sturdy enough, but he stepped up on it cautiously. He had little reason to trust the blonde with his safety.

"Stick your chicken-ass cock between her breasts. You won't fall unless you lose control. The chair is perfectly strong."

"Come on, dick," Andrea said, nearly salivating at the sight of his cock. "Give me that exquisite piece of meat." She jiggled her breasts to show her impatience.

Looking down at her from the chair's height made him slightly dizzy. The aerial view of her cleavage would have made him weak no matter where he stood. His challenge was to remain upright while he enjoyed it.

Knowing she couldn't wait to have his wood between her breasts made him tremble with excitement. Just as he touched his engorged mushroom head to Andrea's ample flesh, the blonde spoke.

"And don't even think about coming. You keep that sticky shit to yourself. Just fuck her until she gets tired of it."

He fought the urge to protest. Naturally, he'd already envisioned spraying thick streams of jism all over Andrea's chest. He imagined it oozing down the curve of each breast, coating the nipples, and dropping off in wet clumps onto the floor. And he even imagined the blonde licking it off her. Guess that fantasy was shot to hell.

"Fuck them," Andrea whispered as he pushed his cock into her warm, eager cleavage. The sweat from both their bodies helped lubricate the action, but it wasn't nearly as good as pussy juice might have been. He toyed with the idea of telling Andrea to provide some but decided against it.

He fucked those big, beautiful breasts slowly, careful at first not to lose his balance. Andrea moved forward and did her best to position herself for his comfort. Her movements protected him from falling but not from coming.

He tried to follow orders but the continuous pumping of those meaty balloons, and Andrea's ongoing encouragement— "yeah, that's right, fuck my titties, look at 'em shake for you, my breasts are eating your big cock, oooooh yes, fuck my big fuckin' tits"—didn't help. He held back as long as he could, but the blonde wouldn't let him squeeze the base of his cock, which was the only way he knew to stall an orgasm. Instead, he let fly with a load of come so heavy, he groaned when it erupted.

"Yes! Oh yes, baby. Come on my breasts. Cover my breasts with it, that's right," Andrea said while she pushed her dripping breasts into his balls.

The blonde stood by, hands on her hips, eyes aflame. "You're just aching for punishment, aren't you?" she demanded. "You're so fucking stupid, I can't believe it. You did exactly what I told you not to do," she said, shaking her head, incredulous at his behavior.

"Get off the chair, you idiot," she commanded. "Kneel before us."

He got down as quickly as his weak and quivering knees would allow. Once he knelt before them, inhaling the rich sweetness of stereo pussy, the blonde continued.

"I'm going to feed you your own come. And you're going to

swallow it. Got it?" She looked down at him like he was a cockroach in her kitchen.

Her manicured fingers scooped up globs of his come from Andrea's chest, which she then put in his mouth and told him to eat. He winced at the bitter saltiness he'd spewed all over Andrea, but he ate his own come as commanded.

The Mistress stroked Andrea to ensure that every drop was scraped off her body and deposited into his mouth.

"Disobey me again and you'll be licking up more than just your own come," the Mistress threatened with that steely quality in her voice. Then she turned, beckoned to Andrea to gather his clothes and the rug, and they left him alone in the black room.

Other than a long, mournful glance back at Victor, Andrea obeyed the Mistress without protest.

The dungeon grew darker as one of the candles burned itself down to a puddle of wax. With nothing to sit on—the chair had been taken along as well—he tried to make himself comfortable on the inhospitable cement. Between the frigid floor and his tensing muscles, his cock had nearly withdrawn into his body. Hunger had long since become a memory, replaced by cold as the dominant sensation.

Finally, after what seemed like several days, the icicle-blond Mistress walked back in as if she'd only stepped out for a cigarette break. She wore the tiniest black silk thong he'd ever seen and those signature stiletto heels.

He tried to scramble to his feet, but she loomed above him before he could get upright. Her Amazonian frame towered over him—big, firm, naked breasts that would have beckoned on any other woman kept him at a safe distance. The expression on her face, a cross between disdain and intolerance, kept him quiet.

"Your cock has shriveled," she observed with those jade-colored watchdog eyes.

He looked down at the organ in question. "I wouldn't say that," he said, instinctively defending his trusty skin flute. "Mistress," he added hastily.

"I doubt it'll ever get hard again," she pronounced.

He took the little shrunken tube between his fingers to examine it and hopefully bring it to life.

"What are you doing?" she snapped. "Did I say you could touch it?"

"No, Mistress."

"No matter what happens, you may not touch your cock. If that's what you call it," she sneered at the retiring flesh between his legs. "Even if I do this."

She moved the slim strip of silk to one side, exposing her succulent cunt. Was she always wet or did the sight of his abbreviated manhood arouse her?

He continued to look up, feeling smaller and hornier by the second. The long, smooth expanse of her toned legs, stretching upward, made him dizzy. He longed to move between her legs and bury his face in her snatch. The thought stirred his cock, which flopped against his thigh as it prepared for growth.

She slid a long, feminine finger along her pussy lips, spreading her juice with each movement. Her eyes never wavered from his. "I absolutely forbid you to touch yourself," she reiterated.

The sound of her wet pussy reverberated off the walls of the dungeon, echoing in his consciousness like some primal mating call. She nearly dripped she was so wet. The scent of her was so alluring, he sat on his hands to keep them away from her as well as from himself.

Her other hand squeezed and kneaded her big, round breasts,

and she was careful to keep the nipple exposed between her fingers so he could see how hard, pink, and begging to be sucked it was. She closed her eyes as she played with her beautiful, luscious body. Her hips gyrated in a rhythm she dictated as she dispensed her own pleasure. He knew she got off on being watched and yet he felt completely invisible.

She opened her eyes suddenly and looked at his cock to make sure he wasn't touching it. Despite the pain involved in following her orders, he dutifully kept his hands away from his now fully erect dick.

She turned around, bent over, and continued to play with her cunt. Now, though, he not only had a different view of her swollen pussy lips but also had the opportunity to stroke his aching rod. As she beat herself to a froth, he snuck in a quick grab of his meat. When that went unnoticed, he stole another opportunity, then another, until finally, he was beating himself off like the sick fuck he knew himself to be.

Of course, she caught him.

"You impertinent little dickhead," she growled. Her breasts were still bouncing from turning around so quickly to face him. "Your pleasure will not be worth your punishment." She took her hand away from her blond beaver and placed both hands on her shapely hips.

"Damsels!" she shouted.

Six women, all blonde, all dead ringers for the Mistress, surrounded him. Though their heights varied somewhat, they were all busty and dressed only in black boots that ended at mid-thigh. Each of them wore fluorescent pink silicone dildos strapped to their hips, and held them in their hands, ready to use them.

"This pervert was whacking off when I told him not to. Administer punishment."

Damsel One grabbed his hair to steady his head. Damsel Two slapped his face with her dildo before she force-fed it into his mouth. He nearly gagged at the force and taste of it but Damsel Two paid no attention. She fucked his mouth with long, hard thrusts until the Mistress told her to stop. He coughed for nearly a minute, hoping to earn some sympathy.

"Fuck his idiot ass," the Mistress commanded.

Damsel Three, with a strength that exceeded that of most men, flipped him over onto his stomach. Damsel Four pulled his hips upward, spread his cheeks, and slapped them with one loud gesture. A pause followed. Nobody moved. Was everybody staring at his upturned ass? He dared not turn around to look.

Damsel Five poured something slick between his cheeks and rubbed it into his crack—not like a lover but more like a no-nonsense masseuse preparing her client for a rubdown. His chest was against his knees. Whatever she poured on him (was it oil?), dripped onto his calves.

Damsel Six approached him from behind. Her dildo tapped his ass, like it was a microphone being tested. He felt fingers at his asshole, cramming their way inside. When two of them were in, they wiggled and he groaned. Damsel Six wasted no time in spreading his cheeks, removing her fingers, and jamming the dildo up his ass so suddenly that he shouted in delicious pain.

She fucked him hard, slowly at first, but then fast. Everything inside him felt torn and wide open. She didn't care. His cock bobbed and even twisted somehow as the flashes of pain melded with waves of hot, burning pleasure. When he felt he might weep with overstimulation, his cock spewed endless streams of come up onto his chest and face. The women laughed and Damsel Six relentlessly rammed his ass until he lost track of where he was and what was happening.

Victor remained in his dungeon, punished sometimes hourly

and sometimes not at all for days. Each time Mistress started to feel he had expunged his guilt and told him he would soon be free to leave, Victor would weep and beg. Mistress remained unmoved and would have Andrea bring his clothes down to him. Victor, each time, would purposefully break a taboo set by Mistress, thus prolonging his stay and earning him new punishments. In the end, Mistress was gone long before Victor, who outlasted all the damsels of the dungeon.

Michael Clark

JennaTip #12: Do-It Yourself Dungeons

In BDSM play, a dungeon is any space set aside for bondage, domination, and sadomasochistic activities (hence BDSM) and may or may not be an underground, dark, dismal, cell with chains and whips. It might be a storage closet. It isn't really where it is or even how it is decorated that makes it a dungeon, it is why it exists that makes it one. It exists as a place for spanking and whipping, biting, and humiliating. It exists for pleasure, even if it's painful.

With that in mind, it isn't so hard to set up a dungeon in a little apartment even when you have kids and occasionally need a spare bedroom for your mother-in-law. Because the dungeon is a state of mind as much as a physical space, a few choice items, a little specially chosen color, just the right sort of bed frame and flooring, can make a space that at certain times is nothing more than a little extra room and at other times a playroom for adult activities.

First, create your dungeon in a room with a door that locks. This is very important for what would seem obvious reasons.

If there is a window, then get really heavy drapes in a dark color or have some made that are easy to put up for playtime and take down for the rest of the world.

If there is a closet, put a lock on it if you intend to store your toys, gear, and dress-up clothes in it. Consider a chest with a lock as an alternative. Most Lane hope chests come with a lock and key, though I don't think the original intent was to hold latex bodysuits, shackles, and ball gags.

Put removable hooks into the ceiling for hanging nice large ferns when not hanging your submissive partner.

Just as certain older houses have had ironing boards installed into the walls that fold down after the little door is opened or even Murphy beds (the beds that are up in the walls and fold down for usage) are making a comeback, well, with a little imagination and a little ingenuity, this same concept can be used for certain tables that a dom might very well wish to use.

So you see, even in a little space a nicely outfitted dungeon can be made as long as your mind and imagination are large enough.

Eastern rituals are some of the most sensual rituals in the world and cleanliness is next to sexiness.

The Cleansing

One soft light along the dark mountain road suggested the entrance to the Kabuki baths. In his anxiety, he almost missed the driveway, which led him another quarter mile in semidarkness until the low roof of the bathhouse emerged.

Bonsai trees cut strange and misshapen figures in the moonlight. The scent of star jasmine filled the night with a feminine presence, at once stimulating and calming. He breathed deeply as he traversed the tranquil garden on his way to the front door.

Inside, dim light recreated the night he'd left outside, and he wondered briefly if he was really inside. He looked up to see if stars were visible. They were not.

A stunningly beautiful geisha appeared from behind a screen. Smiling and gracious, she spoke his name in greeting and with a slow, subtle nod, she directed him to follow her. They walked wordlessly through a lantern-lit maze of hallways where only quiet, insistent streams trickled and flowed through small fountains tucked into the walls.

The petite geisha moved with feline refinement, her bottom swaying just enough to make him watch a little longer. She stopped suddenly and stood by a teakwood door, inviting him with her eyes to open it.

Candles afloat in clear bowls of water lined the perimeter of the sparse but spacious room. A rice-paper screen partly shielded him and the geisha from the steamy sunken bath at the back. A hint of citrus tickled his nostrils. In the center of the room, a wide, backless wooden bench sat alongside a pink-robed Japanese woman, who sat demurely with eyes lowered.

"Ancient Japanese custom says a man must be cleansed before he may partake of the hot bath," the geisha explained. Her English, though heavy with a Japanese accent, was both charming and precise.

"Is there somewhere I can go to shower?" He wanted to respect Japanese tradition and enter the bath as clean as he needed to be.

"No. No shower," she shook her head. "Please remove your clothes and then you will lie down here. Ichiko will wash you."

Ichiko's eyes remained on some indeterminate speck on the wooden floor. He paused, then began to disrobe.

The geisha, hands clasped demurely at her waist, watched him with neither challenge nor encouragement. As he undressed, her expression did not change.

Soothing warmth met his naked skin as his clothes dropped to the floor. The geisha retrieved them, one by one, draping them over her arm as if they were emperor's finery. Though he knew she'd seen many naked men before, he wondered what sort of assessment lurked behind her inscrutable eyes. Still Ichiko would not look up.

"Lie down, please," the geisha said gently. As he complied, she glided over to a wall to hang his clothes on several different hooks.

The moment he was supine, Ichiko leaned slightly to her left, dousing a washcloth in the fragrant water by her side. She sat to his left, at hip level.

As she squeezed a small amount of water up the length of his arm, he noted how its temperature matched that of his skin so that all he felt was a wet caress on one arm, then the other.

Ichiko touched the washcloth to his skin so lightly that he barely felt it.

The geisha returned and stood inches from his feet.

"Ichiko must remove the residue of daily life from your skin," she said as the woman ran the textured cloth up his arm with luxurious slowness.

"But she must do so slowly and with great care, for this exterior film of your life has accumulated over time and must be eliminated delicately to prevent disturbance of yin and yang."

His arms, now tingling and weightless, seemed more real to him than the rest of his body.

Ichiko dipped into her basin once more and now dedicated herself to smoothing and sloughing his leaden feet. At the first stirrings of an erection, he stole a glance first at Ichiko, then the geisha. Neither woman showed any sign of disapproval. Indeed, he couldn't be certain they'd even noticed.

The warm water snuck between his toes and slithered down the soles of his feet. She released only the amount necessary from her washcloth to awaken his pores. What coated his feet felt thicker than water and infused with light. He tried to watch, half-expecting to see some ethereal glow below his ankles. The washcloth deftly explored the tender skin between his toes.

"As the poisons of this life leave your skin, the essence of your being rises to the surface. Notice how it demands your attention."

Ichiko's washcloth now tended to his shins. She moved to follow the intricate crags and slopes of his knees with astounding tenacity. The anticipation of her imminent upward movement made him shudder. His penis inhaled the suspense, expanding, lengthening with excitement. It swelled with an exuberance he'd never before allowed himself to fully experience.

"It is natural for you to become aroused by this cleansing ritual," the geisha purred. "Your mortal life force rests between your legs and responds to all stimuli."

His breathing, though deep, came more quickly in the endless seconds Ichiko spent remoistening her washcloth. When at last it made contact with his skin, water swept down his breastbone and over his stomach. He shot a perplexed glance at her, unable to express his profound disappointment about her target. His erection roared silently.

"To balance soul with mortal life force, your heart must be awakened, too. Feel the weave of Ichiko's cloth as it caresses your chest. Imagine the poisons unable to survive near your heart; picture them rolling off your chest, defeated by the clean, healing water."

As the washcloth traveled over his torso, he floated, serene with vitality.

He closed his eyes. His hard-on filled the room, pulsing in tandem with the steady beat of his heart. Rather than the furtive driving need for satisfaction, this hard-on reveled only in its solid, life-affirming existence. It breathed as he did. It embodied all that he thought, felt, and sensed.

"And now that your life force has gathered and absorbed your essence, it is ready for the ultimate cleansing." The swish of water beside him foretold of his impending, glorious fate.

Ichiko's slim fingers lifted his ball sack with unendurable care. He arched his back as the washcloth made its slippery way around his tight testes. As she gently sloughed away impurities, fiery fluid ran rampant under the tantalizing flow of water.

When her fingertips touched his shaft, sharp shots of light passed before him. He trembled as she wiped. And wiped.

The subtle friction made him want to cry out. From pain?

Joy? He didn't know, didn't care. She missed nothing in her assiduous washing: the ridge between shaft and head, the forgotten skin beneath his pubic hair; she even lingered at the tiny slit at his tip.

Did he imagine the softness of her gaze as she stroked him? Did she share in the intensity of his pleasure?

Habit told him to explode, to spill himself everywhere, especially on the two beautiful women. And yet, he savored this new power that gripped him with sublime totality. Never had he been more alive, hovering as he did now between ultimate control and unbridled vulnerability.

"And now you are prepared for your bath," announced the geisha as the silent Ichiko slipped away.

As the geisha helped him into a white cotton robe, she did not cover the erection that led his way to the bubbling hot bath.

"Now you are ready to appreciate relaxation," she said knowingly.

Oni Nurani

JennaTip #13: Geisha

Geishas have been around since the 1800s; they are trained and expert in many arts including tea ceremonies, dancing, painting, singing, and conversation, and are meant to be a comfort and provide entertainment to men. After World War II the prostitutes of Japan marketed themselves to the American GIs as geishas, much to the shame and dismay of the true geisha.

Today, depending on the city, geishas are viewed as either culturally talented companions or as prostitutes, in part in relation to the modernity of the city itself.

Though traditional geishas are trained in the arts, they also often did take lovers from among the men who would purchase their services.

That the profession of geisha has a sexual element is undeniable, though historically the geisha would take a rich lover to help with the fees of the geisha house, for being a geisha, from the training to the makeup, hair, and clothing, is expensive.

Geishas are experts at massage and also cleansing. What they offer their clients is more than simply sex; they offer perfection in all they do. The geisha will bathe a man, undress him, comb his hair, and massage him. The man is required to do nothing. There is no expectation of him at all as everything depends upon her being perfect in her ability to care for him, entertain him, and serve him.

In the end, the sex is not what the man is paying for when he hires the services of a geisha, easily in the thousands for an evening. It is the care with which his every need is attended.

About Sounds Publishing, Inc.

Sounds Publishing, Inc. was founded in 2004 by the husband-and-wife team of Brian and Catherine OliverSmith with the goal of bringing high-quality romantic and erotic content to life in a variety of media. As the leading provider of romance and erotica in audio, one of the cornerstone principles of the company is to produce healthy, sexy erotica encouraging people to increase romance, intimacy, and passion through fantasy.

About the Editor

M. Catherine OliverSmith is the cofounder and editor-in-chief of Sounds Publishing, a co-venture with her spouse, Brian OliverSmith. She is the editor of hundreds of short stories and more than nine compilations and anthologies, served as editor-in-chief of *The Docket,* the official newspaper of the UCLA School of Law, and is the mother of two beautiful girls.

She would like to thank her husband, partner, lover, and best friend, Brian, for making good on his promise that life would never be boring.

About the Cover Photographer

Photographer Mike Ruiz is best known for his high-impact, colorful celebrity and fashion photography. His artistic objective is to present an upscale fashion edge to sensuality with aspirational images of iconic personas. Of all the celebrities he has photographed—from Kirsten Dunst to Ricky Martin to Christina Aguilera, just to name a few—he says he can count on one hand those that he believes truly possess the special unique magic to light up a camera. Jenna Jameson is one.

A mutual friend introduced Ruiz to Jameson for a spec shoot that turned out to be so successful, Jameson asked Ruiz to create the images for her new series of erotica, JennaTales. "Jenna has this amazing chemistry with the lens," explains Ruiz. "She loves the camera and the camera reciprocates that love. Every shot is beautiful."

Though a majority of his work has been with major magazines like *Vanity Fair* and *Interview* in the U.S., and European publications such as *Italian Elle*, *Arena*, and *Dazed and Confused*, Mike Ruiz has contributed to several books including Dolce and Gabbana's *Hollywood* and Iman's *The Beauty of Color*.

In addition to his editorial assignments, Ruiz has shot advertising campaigns for Sean John, MAC Cosmetics, and Reebok. He worked alongside rapper Lil Kim to create the image for her Royalty watch line and has recently branched out as a director, creating music videos for Traci Lords and Kelly Rowland.

This fall, Mike Ruiz made his feature film directorial debut with *Starrbooty*, a new madcap spy/comedy adventure starring the original supermodel of the world, RuPaul. For more information on Mike Ruiz and his projects, visit his website at www.mikeruiz.com.

PUT DOWN THE BOOK . . . and experience hot, sexy, erotica in a whole new hands-free way!

Sounds Publishing offers a wide variety of short audio erotica via download at www.jennatales.com and other online retailers. Visit www.jennatales.com for a FREE erotic tale from the Sounds Publishing collection today. Browse the several titles available for hands-free enjoyment on your MP3 player, iPod, burned to a CD, or directly on your computer.

Other titles from Sounds Publishing, Inc.
In print:

JennaTales: Erotica for the Woman on Top
Something Blue (January 2008)
Something Borrowed (May 2008)
Happy Endings (September 2008)

In audio:

Dulce Amore	*Tongue & Tied*
Melt Away	*A Lick & a Promise*
Kiss Your Ear	*Bend, Lick, Insert, Send*
Nibbles & Bites	*You've Got Tail*

Share Your Fantasies—Be a JennaTales Contributor!

Why not share your favorite, hottest, and best fantasy with the world? Send Sounds Publishing your short, erotic tale for **Jenna-Tales**, *Erotica for the woman on top* and if it is chosen to be developed into an audio story or included in a future **JennaTales** collection of erotica, receive a **free CD**.

Visit www.jennatales.com for submission guidelines and official rules.

Ask Jenna About . . .

In developing **JennaTips**, *Sex tips for the woman on top,* we want to answer *your* burning questions. Tell us exactly what it is you want. Maybe one of the stories really lit your fire and you want more details about how to act it out. Maybe you're just curious about something you've heard about, read about, seen performed, or imagined.

Visit www.jennatales.com and click on the Ask Jenna! link to e-mail us your question. Keep your eye out for the upcoming **JennaTips**, *Sex tips for the woman on top* books.

Become the woman on top.

Three tasty treats to whet your appetite from Happy Endings, the fourth book in the immensely popular JennaTales series of sexy story anthologies. Whatever you're hungry for, these inventive and entertaining, wickedly wanton stories will feed your imagination.

Tout Parfait

She sat in the upholstered chair until the electric current in her veins dissipated. When she regained control of herself, she slowly slid the stockings up the length of her long legs and attached the garters, pausing to appreciate the luscious weave of the stockings. After a deep and soothing breath, she exited the room, strode to the counter, and paid for her purchases, explaining she had decided to wear the garter belt and stockings.

Her panties remained on the dressing room floor.

Slave for a Night

He lifted the breadbasket. There on the table lay a white envelope with the word *Slave* scrawled on top. There was a small bulge in the envelope. I took the envelope with me into the ladies' room, and ripped it open. There was a note inside. I was astonished by what I read. The note ordered me to tie a piece of black thread around my right nipple and let two feet of thread dangle out of the front of my dress. The bulge in the envelope, I discovered, was a spool of black thread.

Morning Becomes Electra

Remembering the feel of her ice-cold mouth on his, the taste of the mint chocolate chip on her tongue he considered a cold shower for a minute before turning the hot all the way on and watching his mirrors steam up. The heat released the scent of her still clinging to his skin, triggering more memories. He hoped he never lost these crystal-clear memories of her on her knees, of him on his back, of her straddling his face her firm thighs pressing against his ears and her hands flat against the headboard.

*Let these provoking stories entice and electrify you. **JennaTales, erotica for the woman on top** frees your fantasies with **Happy Endings**—coming to a bookstore near you—January 2009.*